STINKY

HEE! HEE!

ELEANOR DAVIS

STINKY

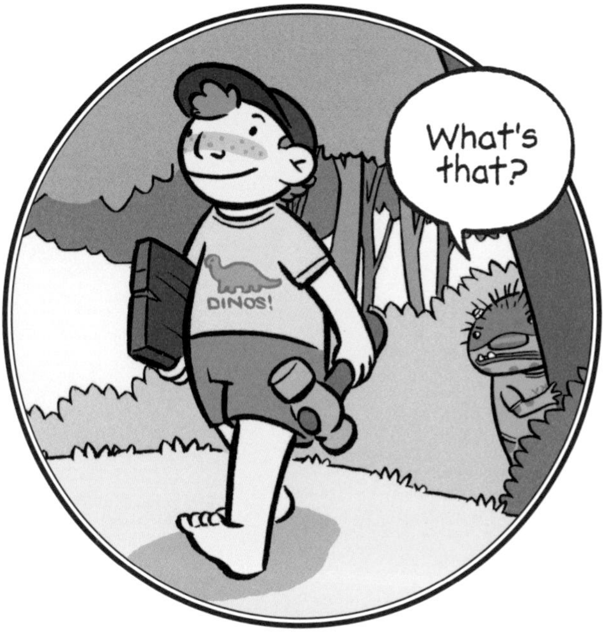
What's that?
DINOS!

A TOON BOOK BY

ELEANOR DAVIS

THE LITTLE LIT LIBRARY, A DIVISION OF RAW JUNIOR, LLC, NEW YORK

Editorial Director: FRANÇOISE MOULY
Advisor: ART SPIEGELMAN

Book Design: FRANÇOISE MOULY & JONATHAN BENNETT

A TOON BOOK

 Library of Congress Control Number: 2007943857

ISBN 13: 978-0-9799238-4-5 ISBN 10: 0-9799238-4-0

10 9 8 7 6 5 4 3 2 1

www.TOON-BOOKS.com

CHAPTER ONE

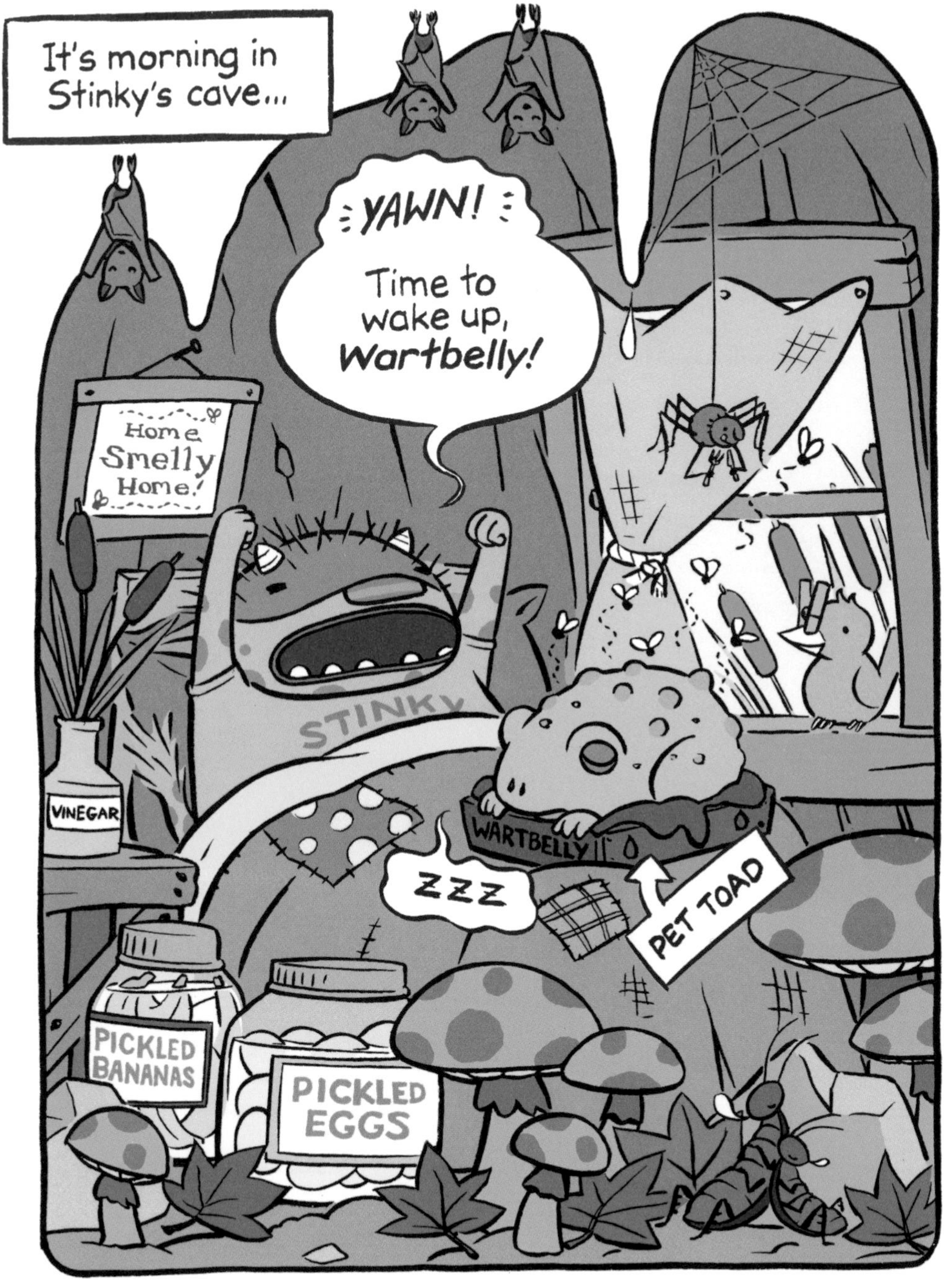

It's morning in Stinky's cave...
YAWN! Time to wake up, Wartbelly!
Home Smelly Home!
STINKY
VINEGAR
WARTBELLY
ZZZ
PET TOAD
PICKLED BANANAS
PICKLED EGGS

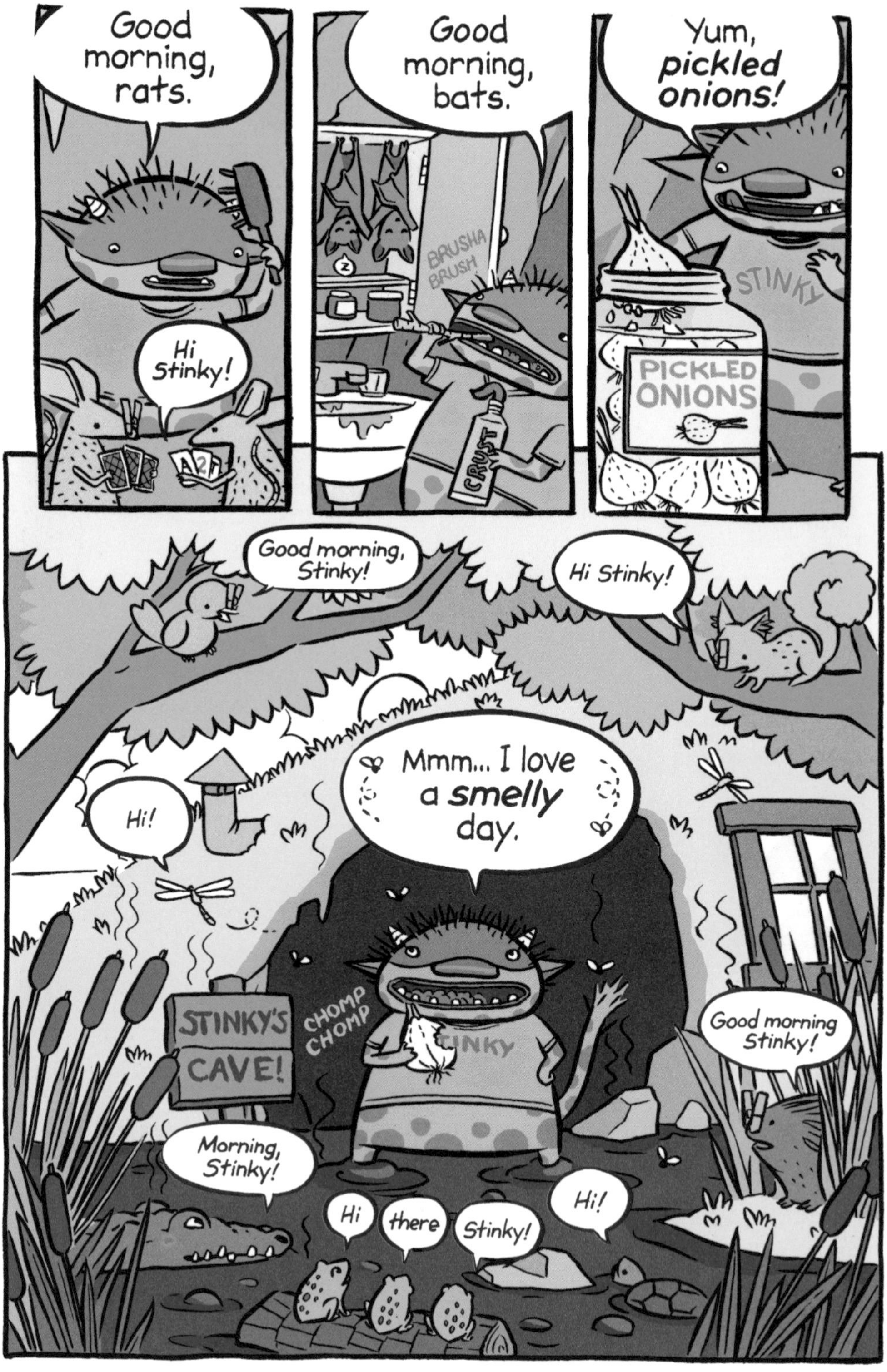
Good morning, rats.
Hi Stinky!
Good morning, bats.
BRUSHA BRUSH
CRUST
Yum, pickled onions!
STINKY
PICKLED ONIONS
Good morning, Stinky!
Hi Stinky!
Hi!
Mmm... I love a smelly day.
CHOMP CHOMP
STINKY'S CAVE!
STINKY
Good morning Stinky!
Morning, Stinky!
Hi
there
Stinky!
Hi!

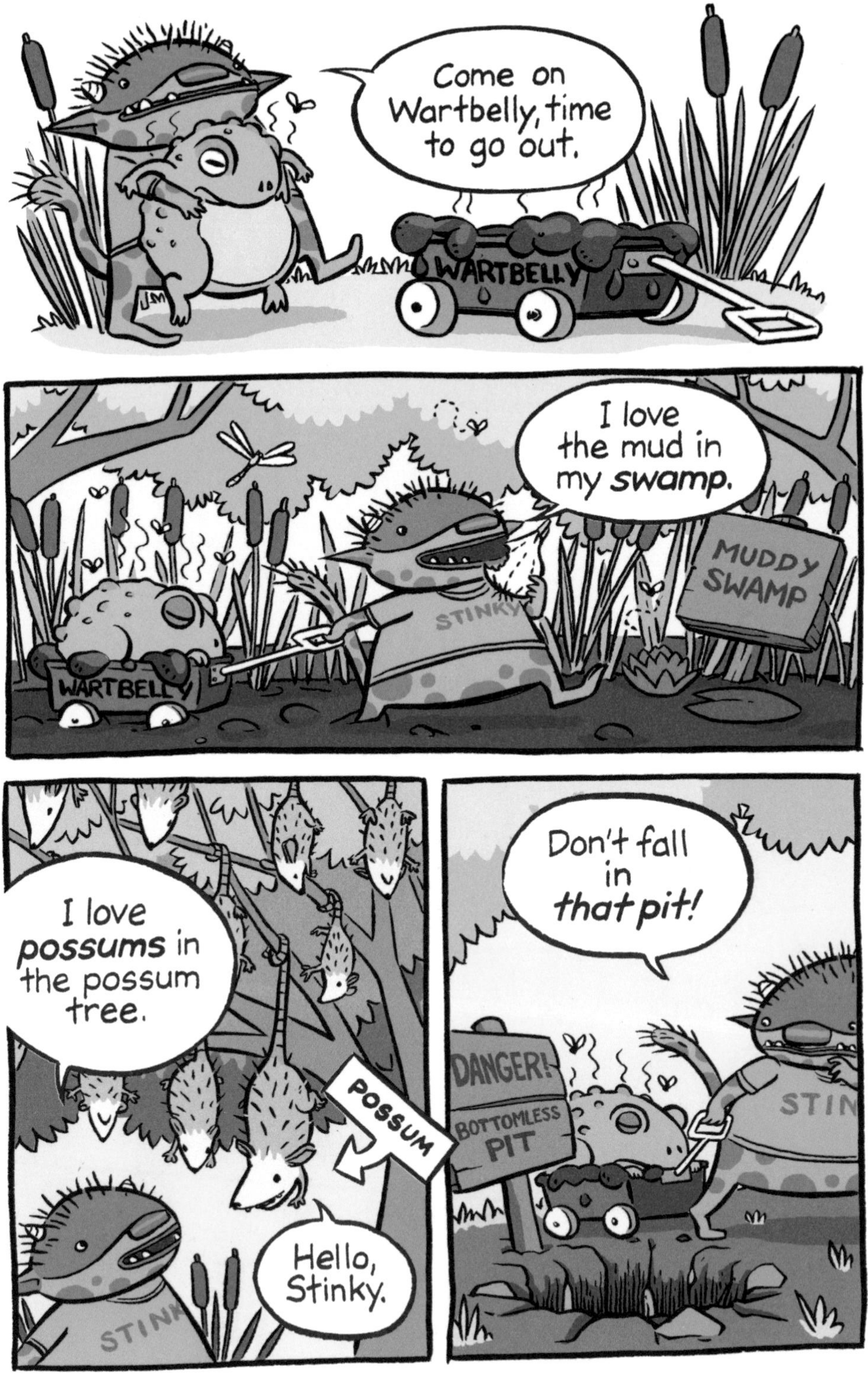

Come on Wartbelly, time to go out.
WARTBELLY
I love the mud in my *swamp.*
MUDDY SWAMP
STINKY
WARTBELLY
I love *possums* in the possum tree.
POSSUM
Hello, Stinky.
STINK
Don't fall in *that pit!*
DANGER!
BOTTOMLESS PIT
STIN

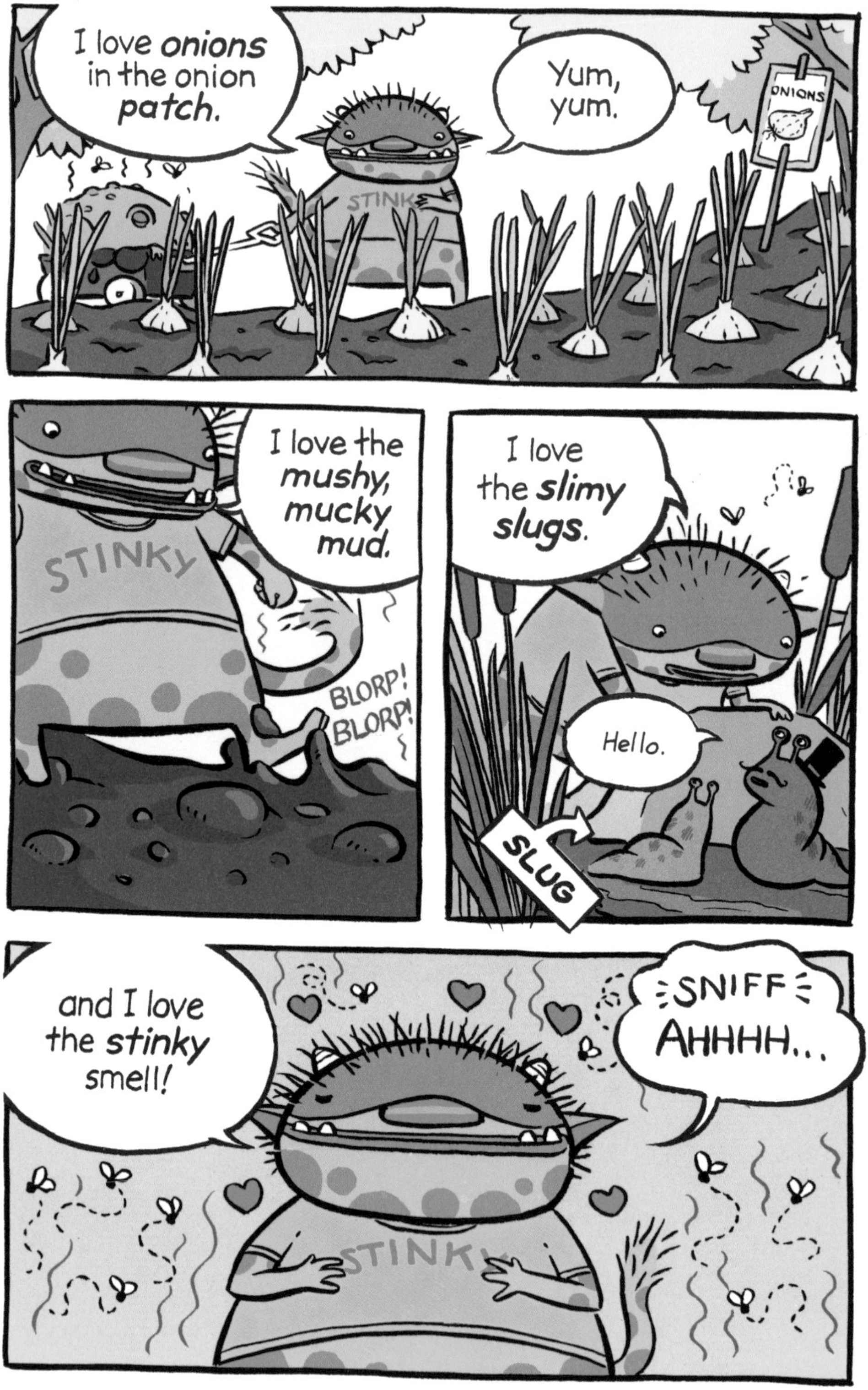
I love onions in the onion patch.
STINK
Yum, yum.
ONIONS
I love the mushy, mucky mud.
STINKy
BLORP! BLORP!
I love the slimy slugs.
Hello.
SLUG
and I love the stinky smell!
SNIFF AHHHH...
STINKy

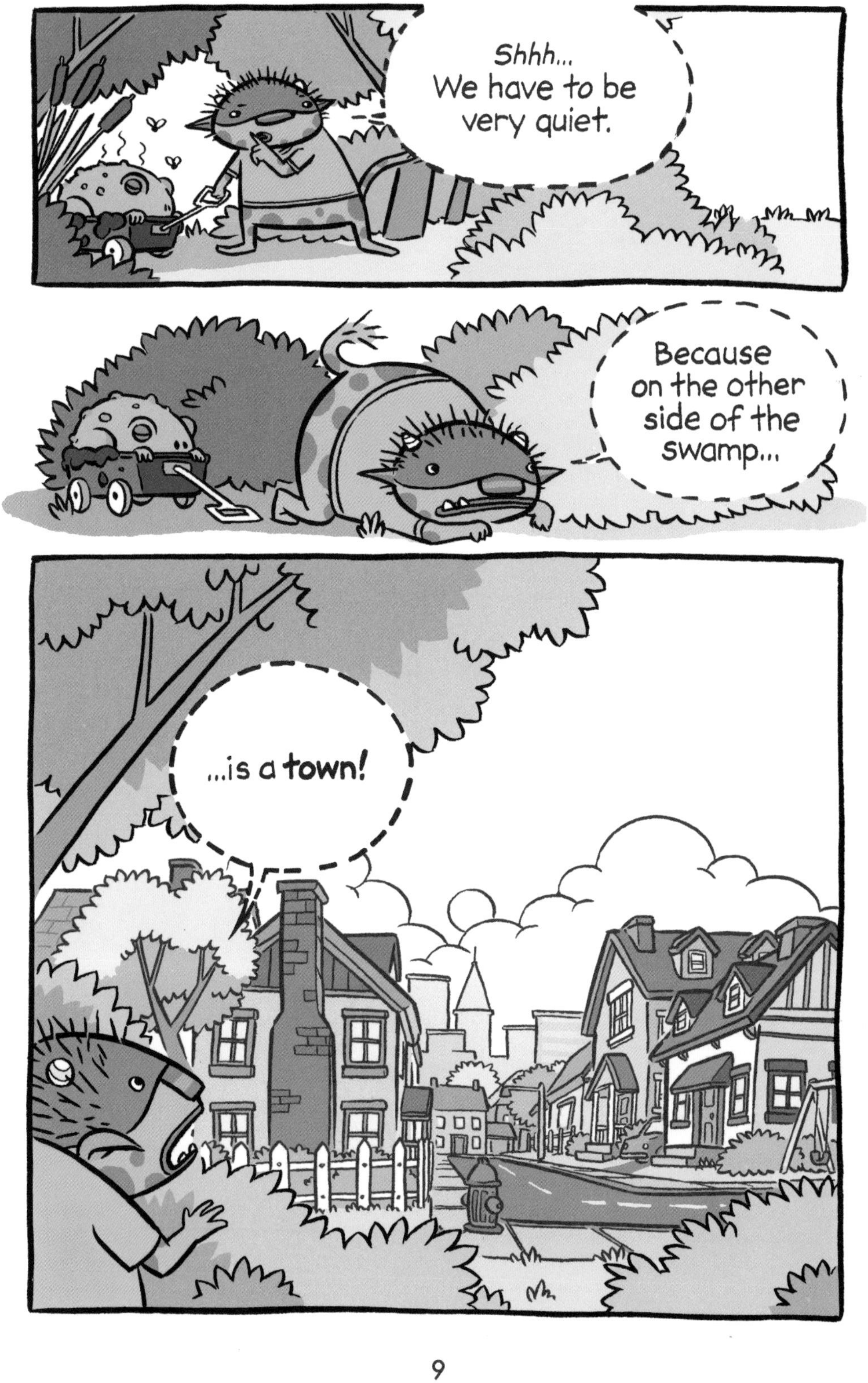
Shhh...
We have to be very quiet.
Because on the other side of the swamp...
...is a **town**!

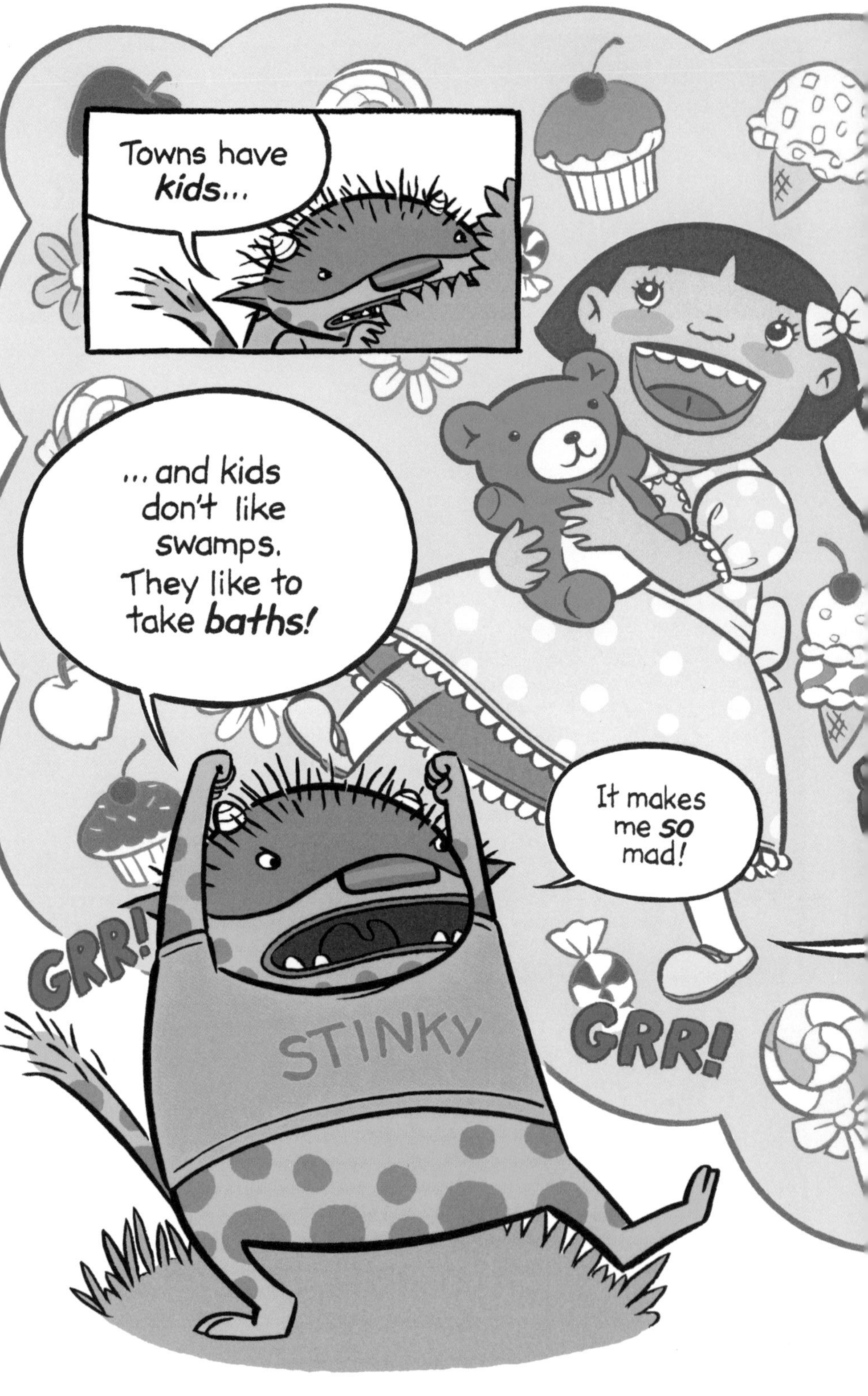
Towns have *kids*...
...and kids don't like swamps. They like to take *baths!*
It makes me *so* mad!
GRR!
STINKY
GRR!

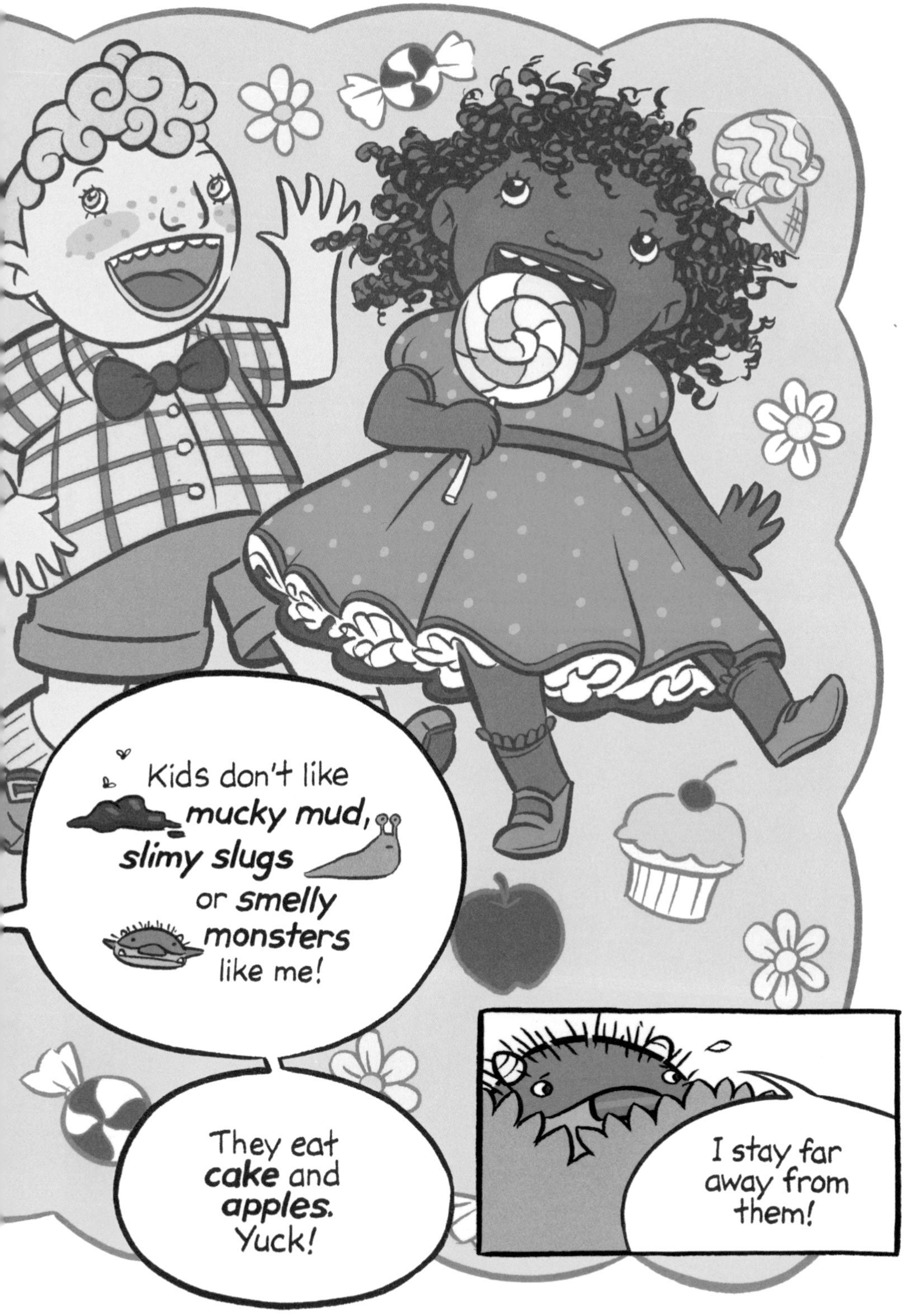
Kids don't like mucky mud, slimy slugs or smelly monsters like me!
They eat cake and apples. Yuck!
I stay far away from them!

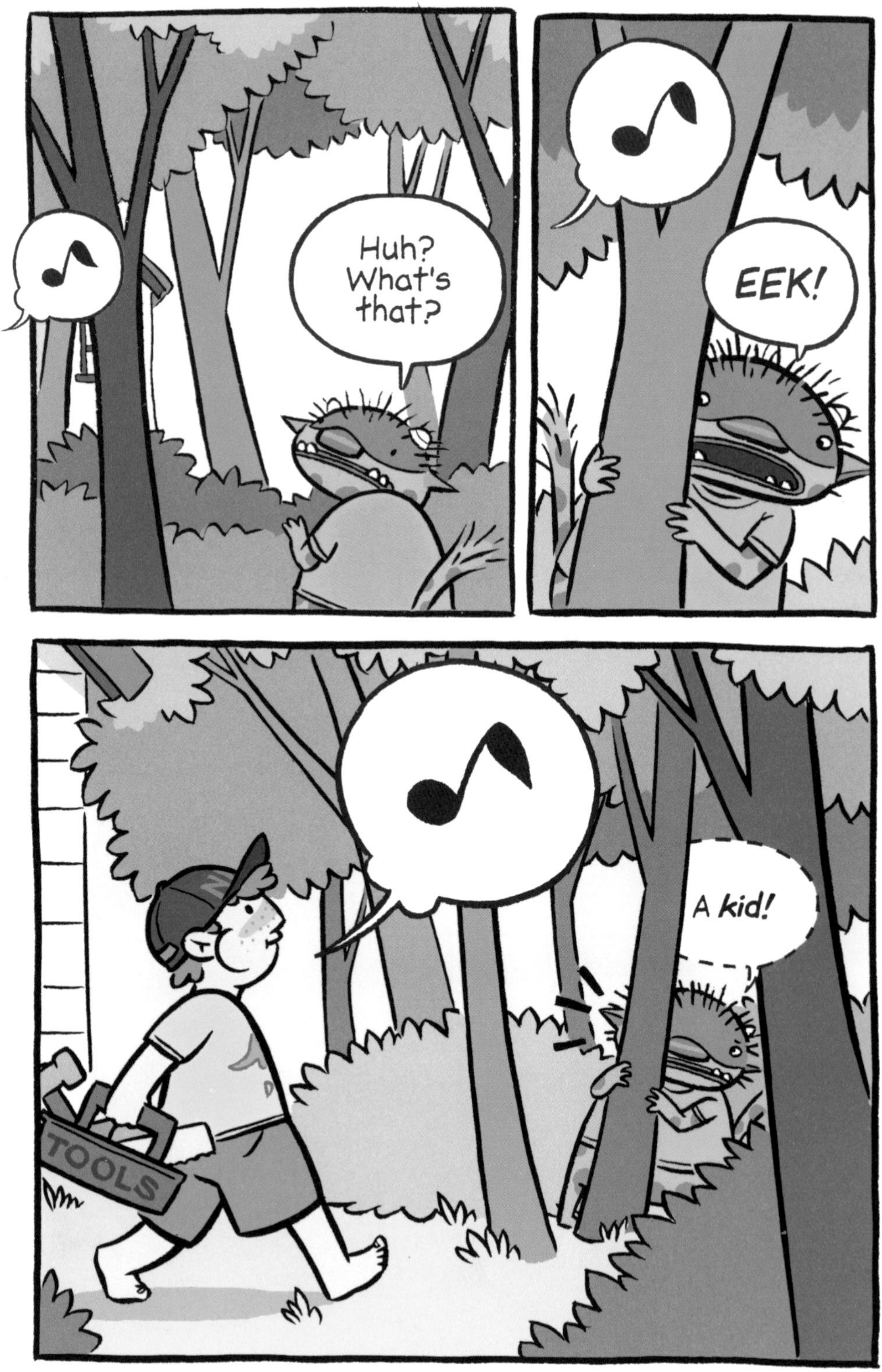
Huh? What's that?
EEK!
A kid!
TOOLS

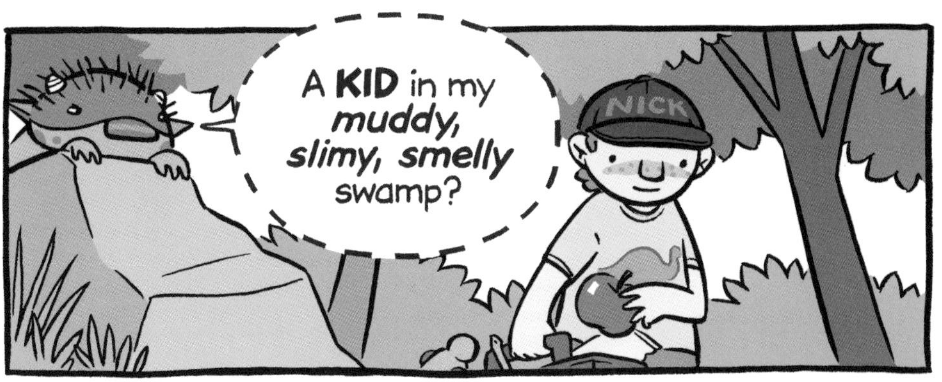
A **KID** in my *muddy, slimy, smelly* swamp?
NICK

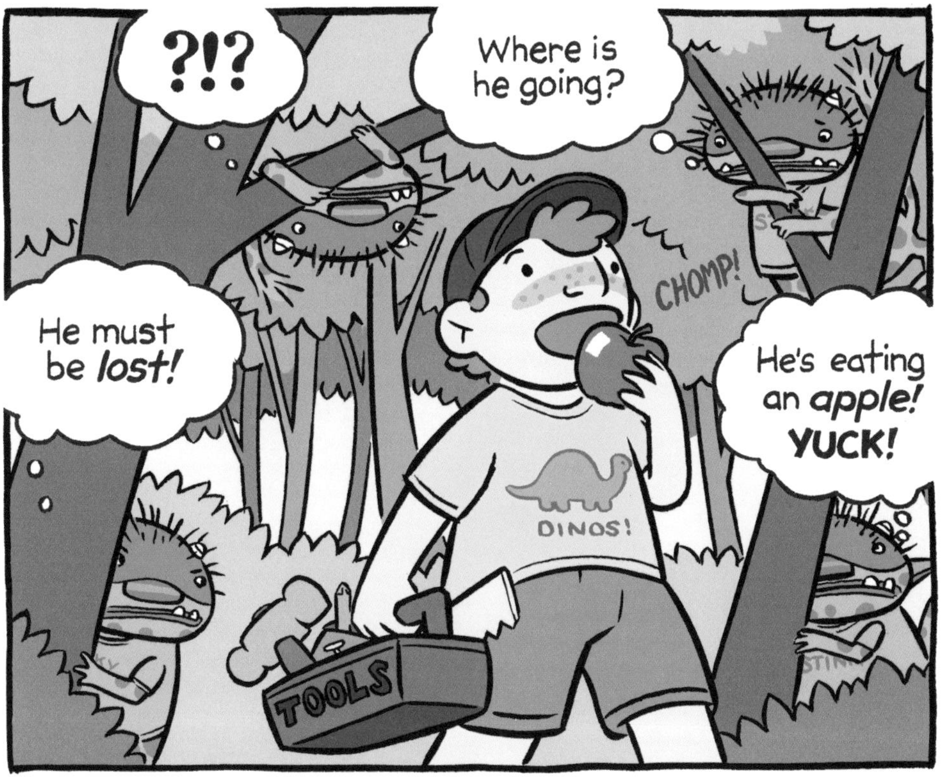
?!?
Where is he going?
He must be *lost!*
CHOMP!
He's eating an *apple!* **YUCK!**
DINOS!
TOOLS

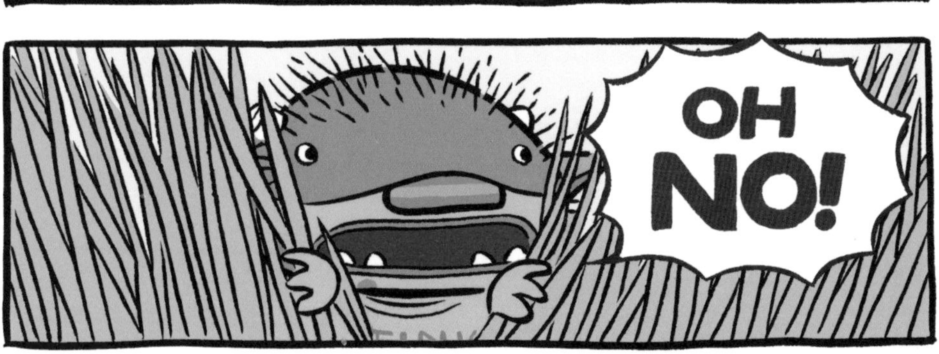
OH NO!

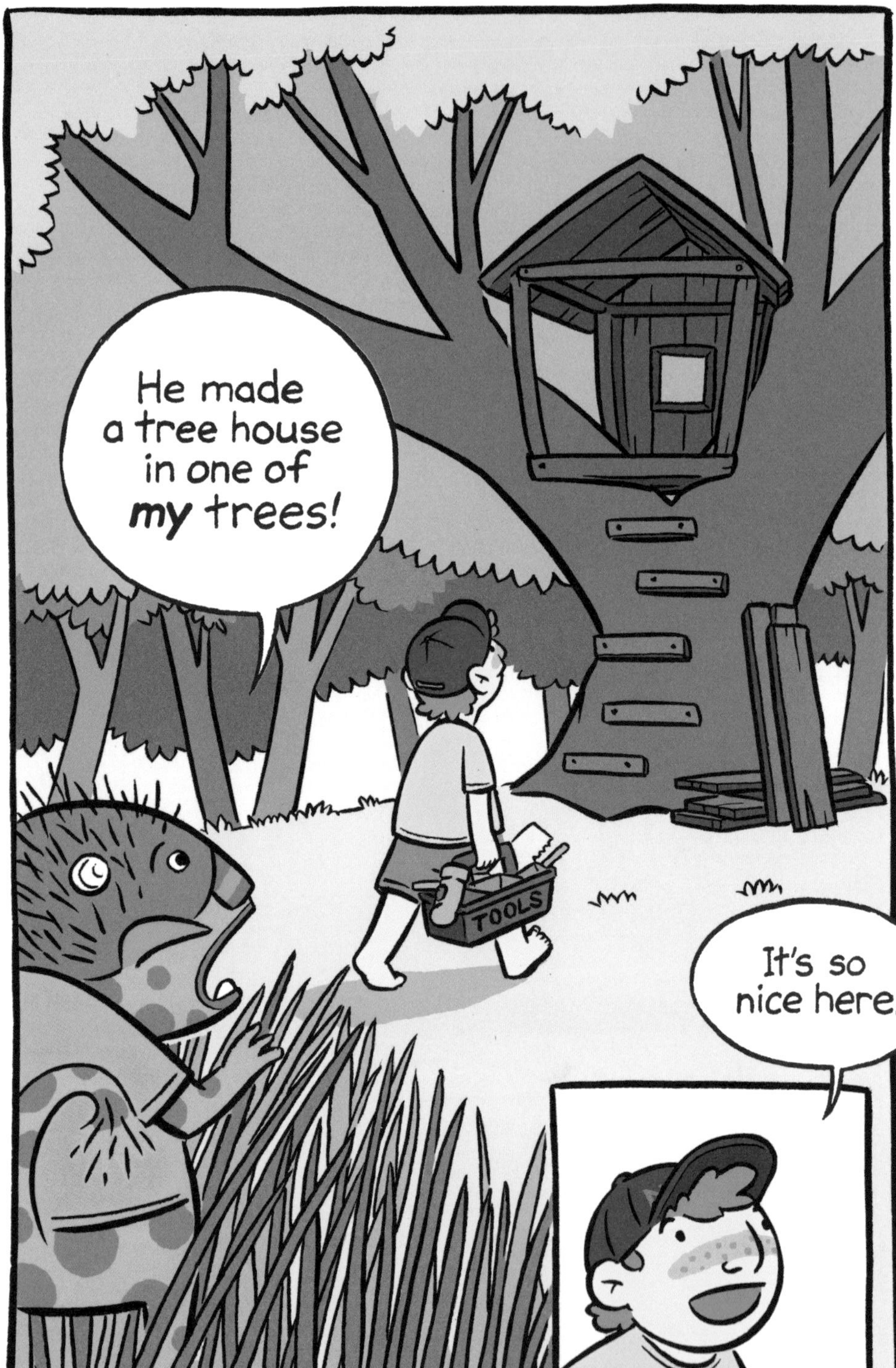
He made a tree house in one of **my** trees!
TOOLS
It's so nice here!

CHAPTER TWO

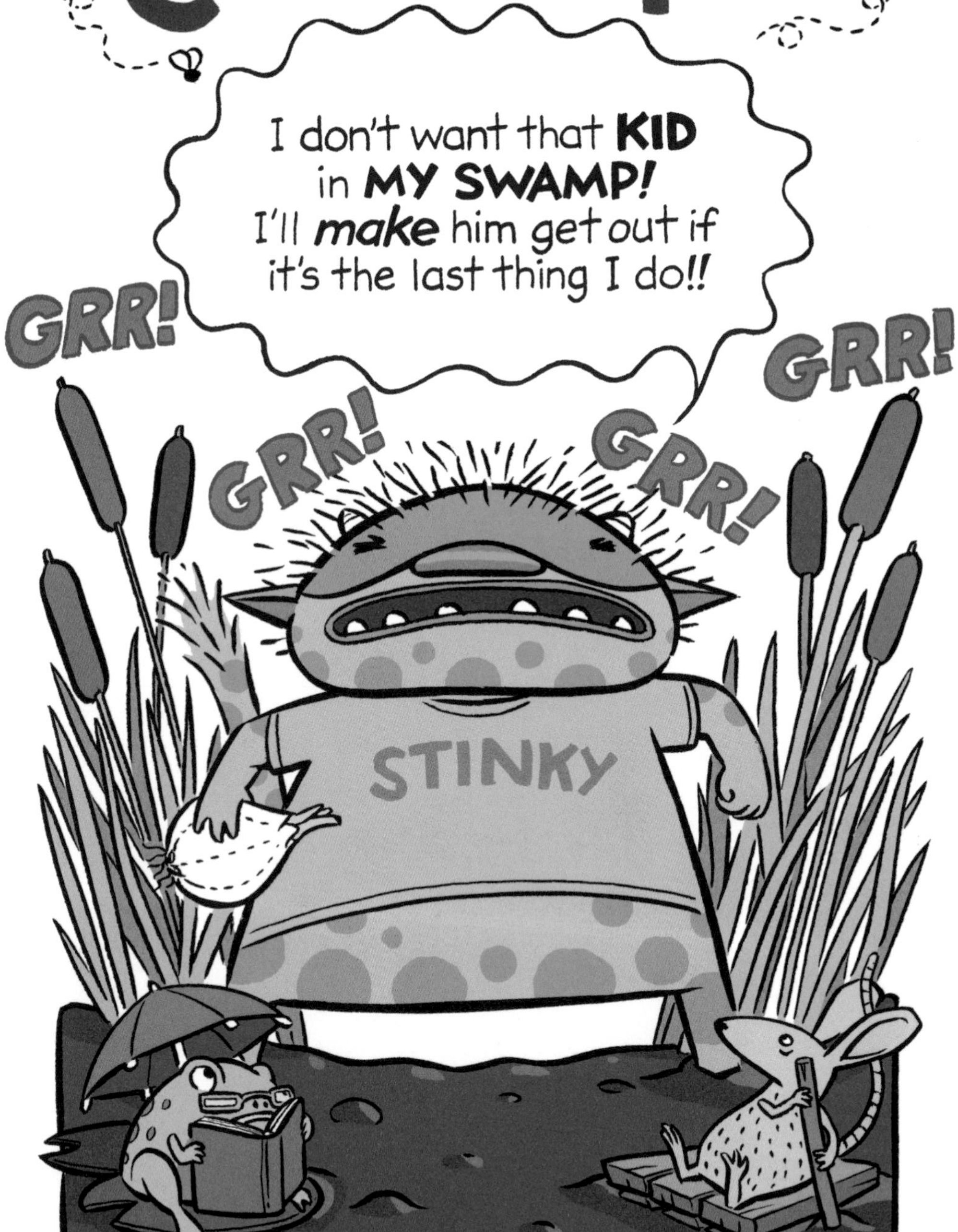
I don't want that **KID** in **MY SWAMP!** I'll ***make*** him get out if it's the last thing I do!!
GRR!
GRR!
GRR!
GRR!
STINKY

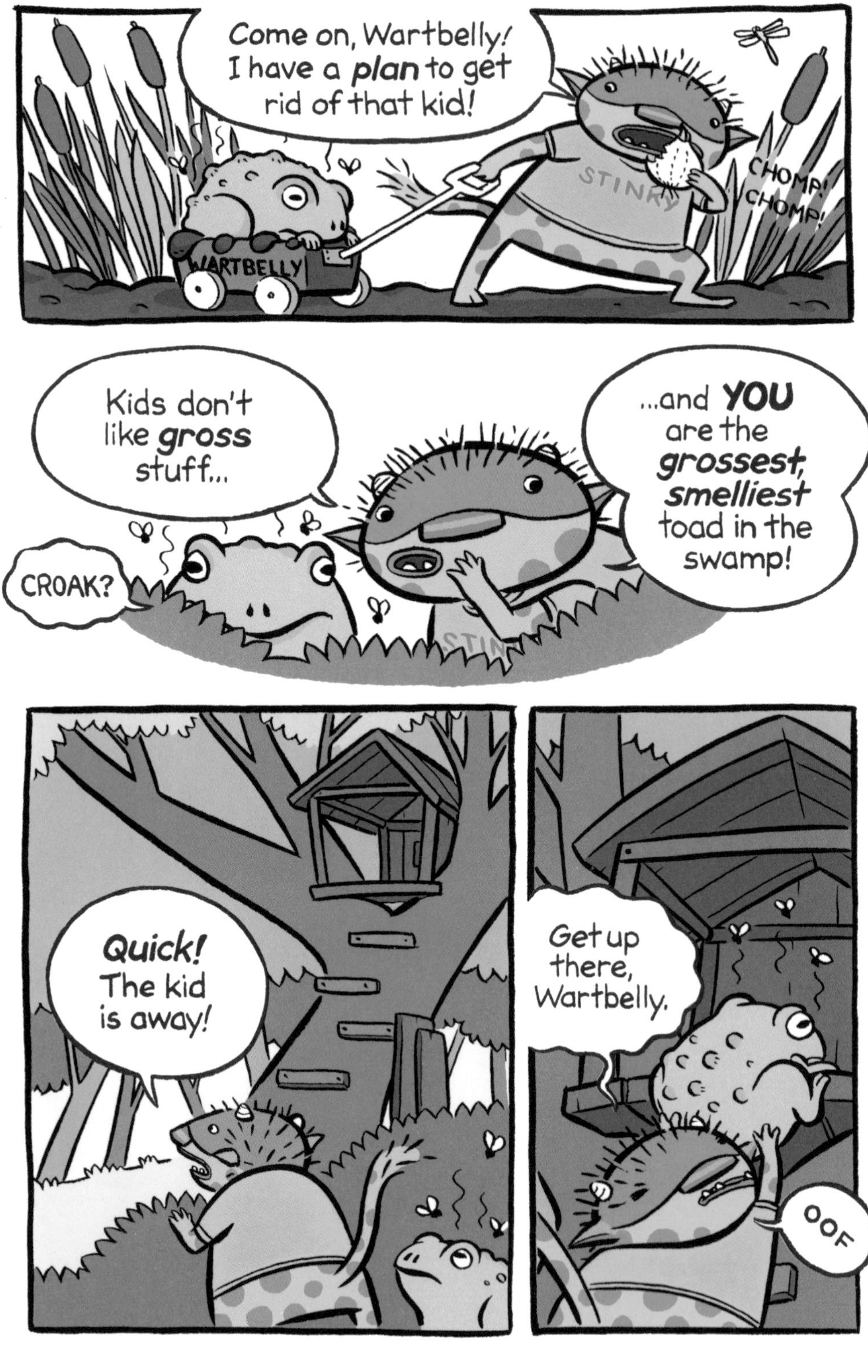
Come on, Wartbelly! I have a plan to get rid of that kid!
WARTBELLY
STINKY
CHOMP! CHOMP!
Kids don't like gross stuff...
CROAK?
...and YOU are the grossest, smelliest toad in the swamp!
Quick! The kid is away!
Get up there, Wartbelly.
OOF

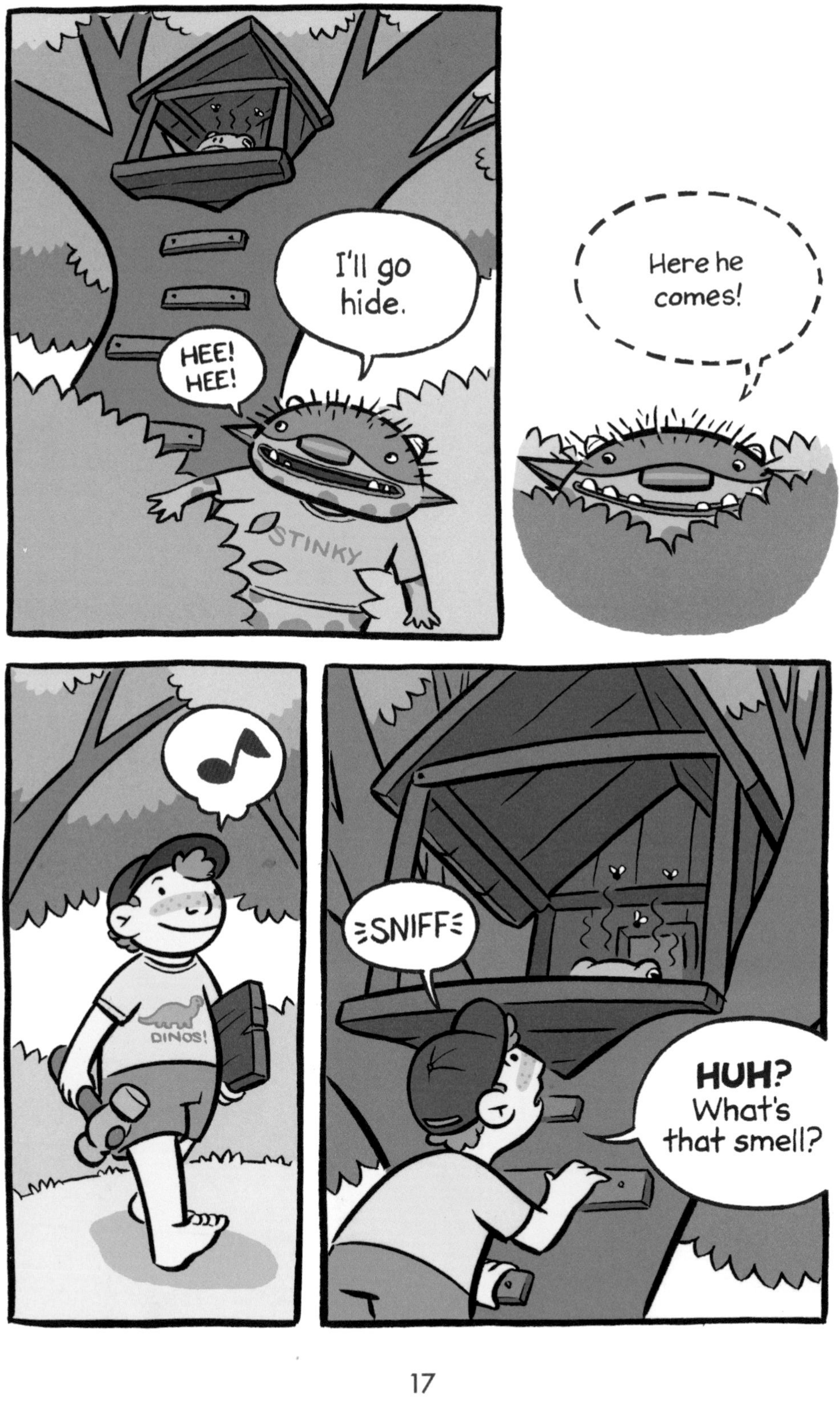
I'll go hide.
HEE! HEE!
STINKY
Here he comes!
DINOS!
SNIFF
HUH? What's that smell?

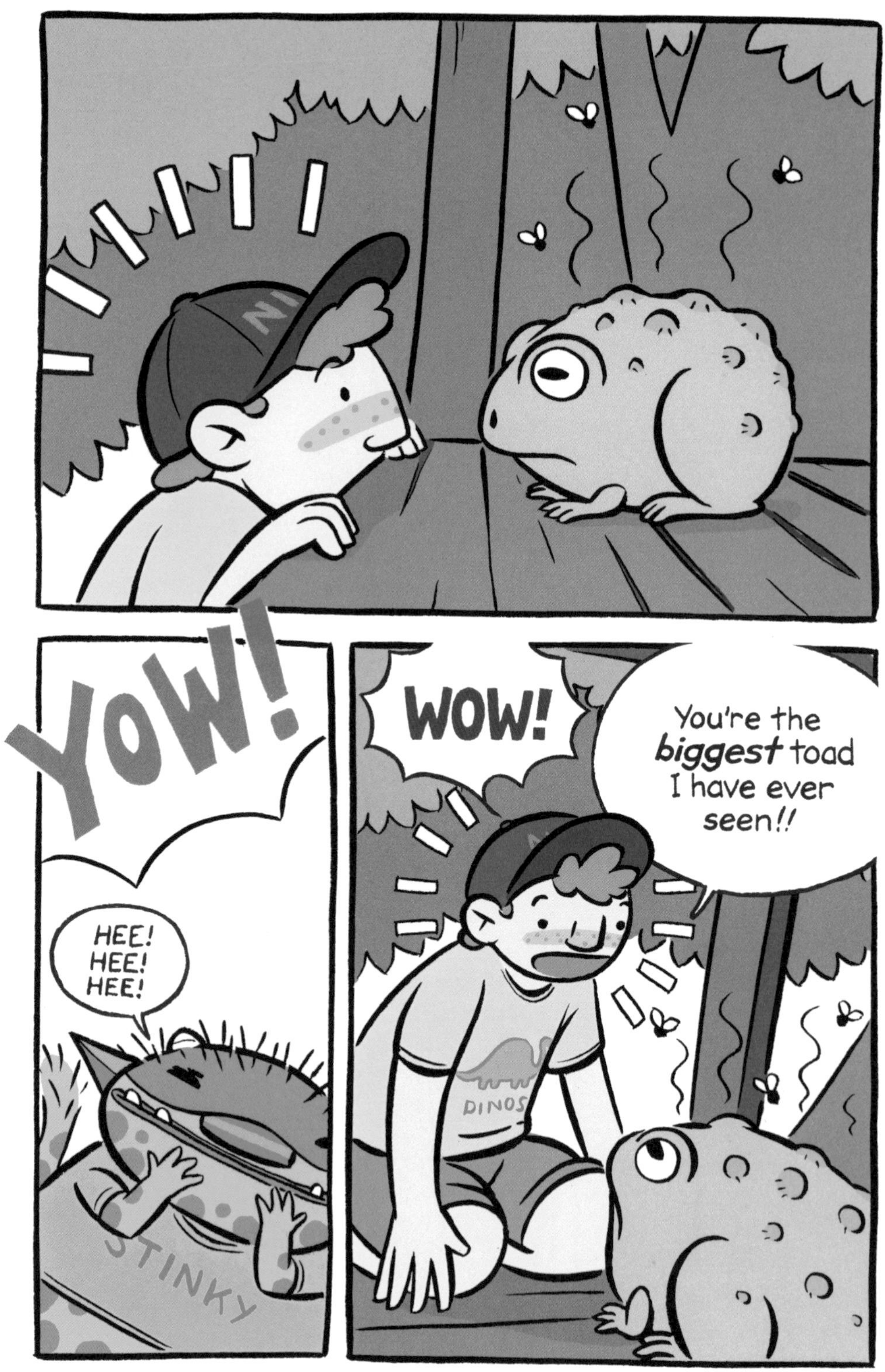
YOW!
HEE! HEE! HEE!
STINKY
WOW!
You're the *biggest* toad I have ever seen!!
DINOS

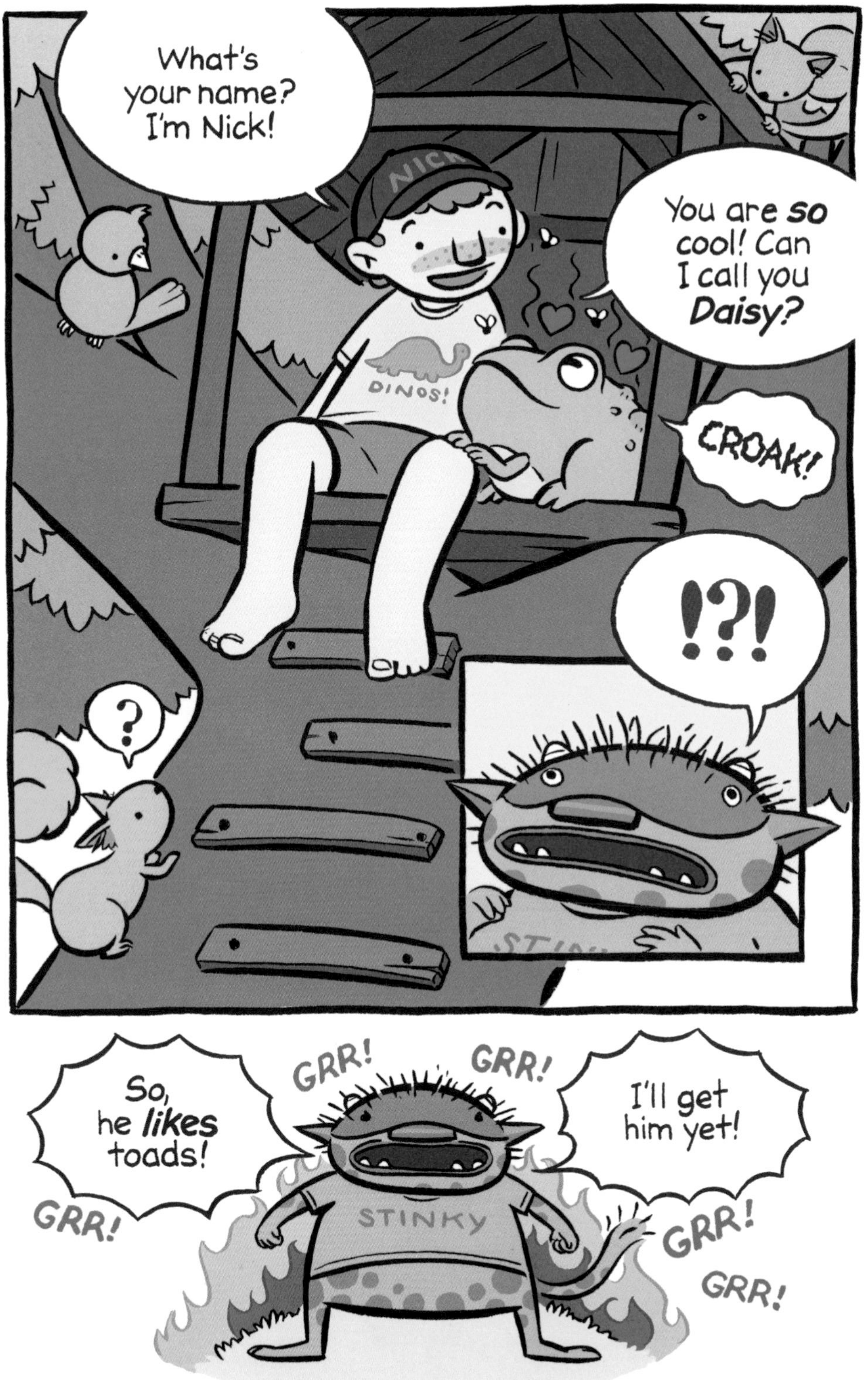

What's your name? I'm Nick!
NICK
You are **so** cool! Can I call you ***Daisy?***
DINOS!
CROAK!
?
!?!
So, he ***likes*** toads!
GRR!
GRR!
I'll get him yet!
GRR!
STINKY
GRR!
GRR!

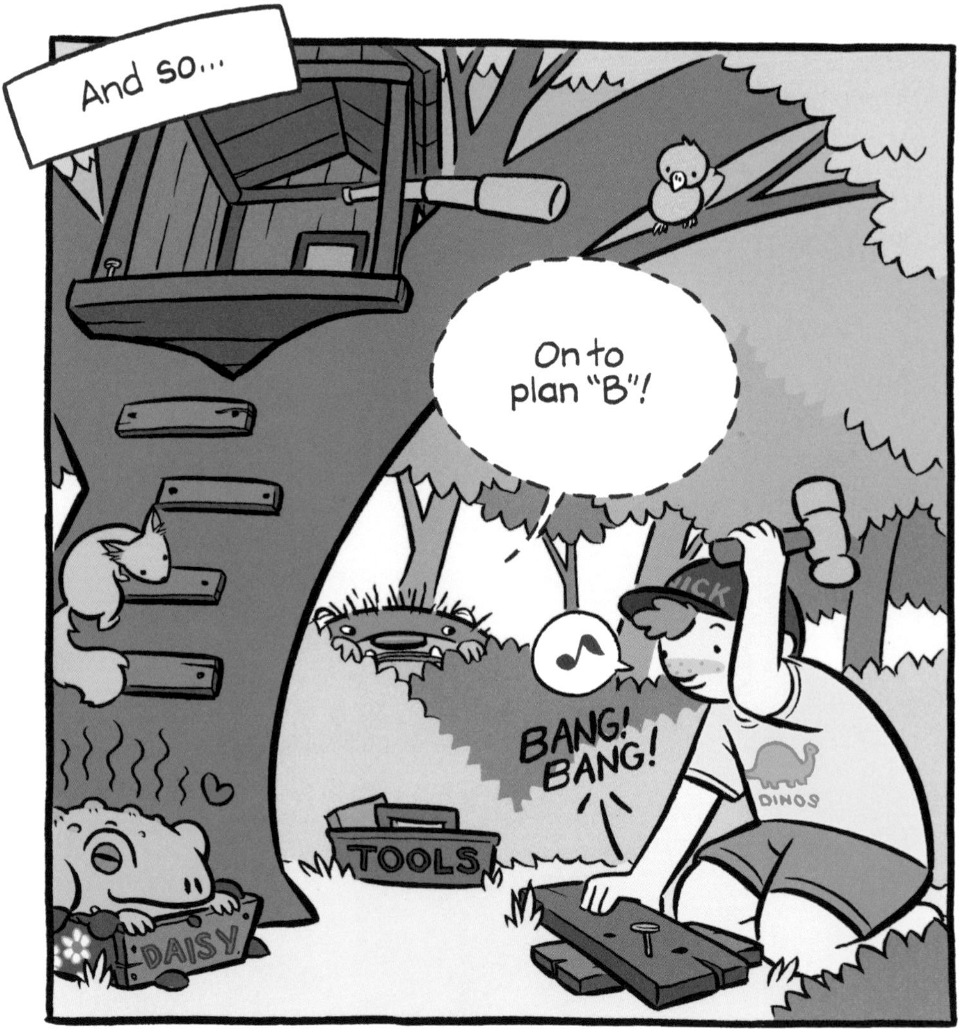
And so...
On to plan "B"!
♪
BANG! BANG!
TOOLS
DAISY
DINOS

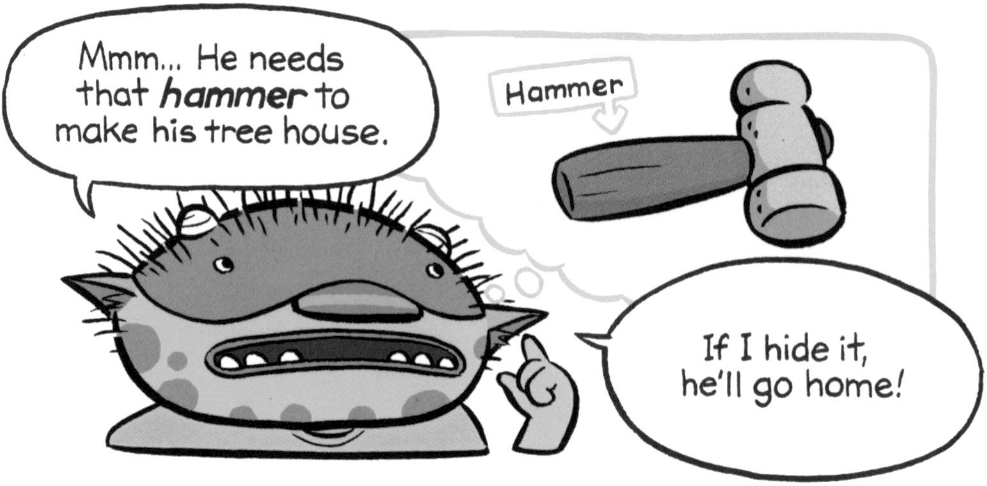
Mmm... He needs that **hammer** to make his tree house.
Hammer
If I hide it, he'll go home!

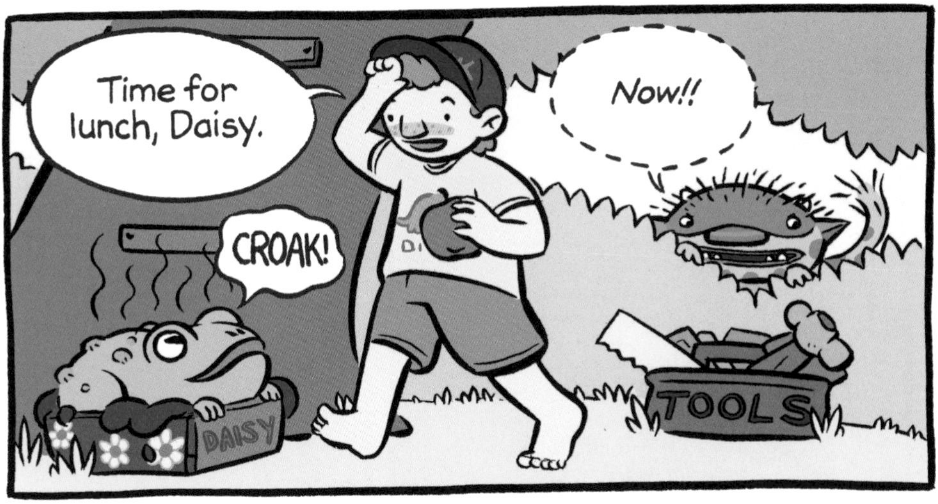
Time for lunch, Daisy.
Now!!
CROAK!
DAISY
TOOLS

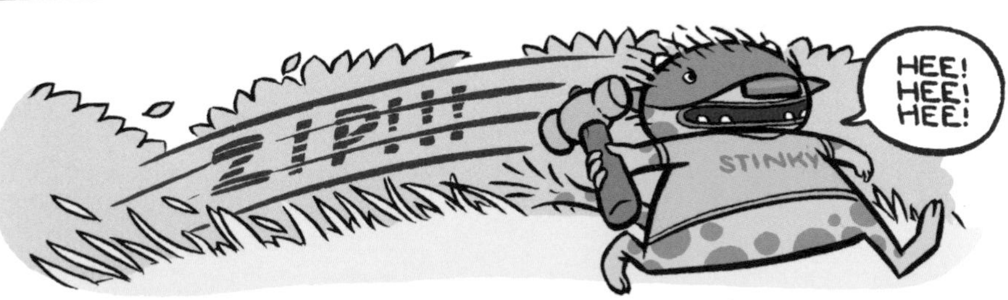
ZIP!!!
HEE! HEE! HEE!
STINKY

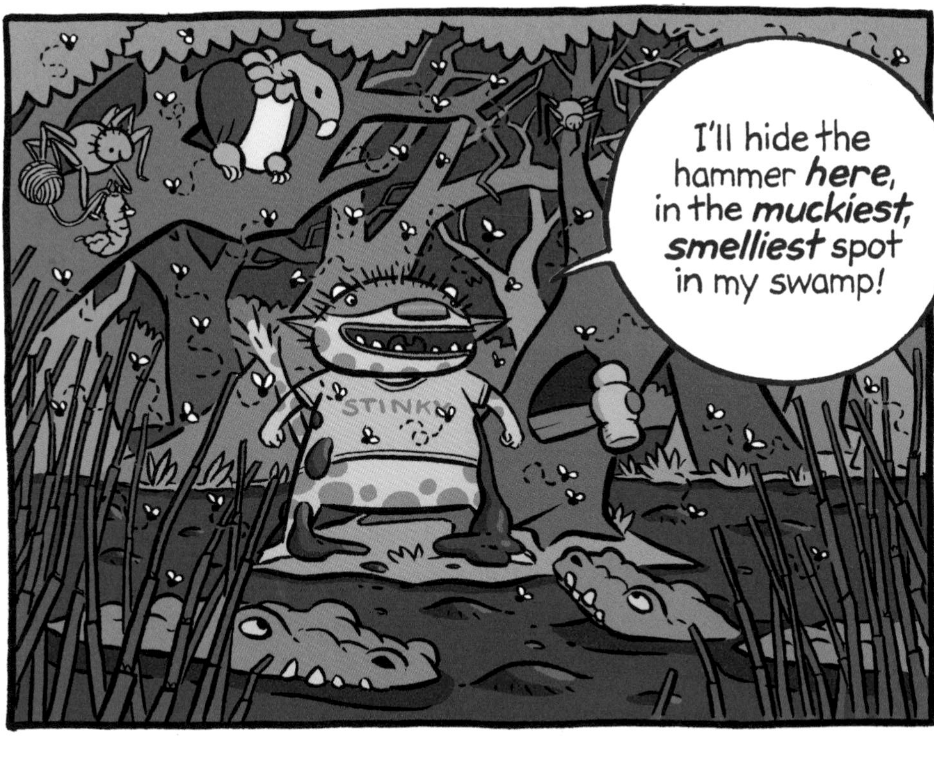
I'll hide the hammer ***here***, in the ***muckiest, smelliest*** spot in my swamp!
STINKY

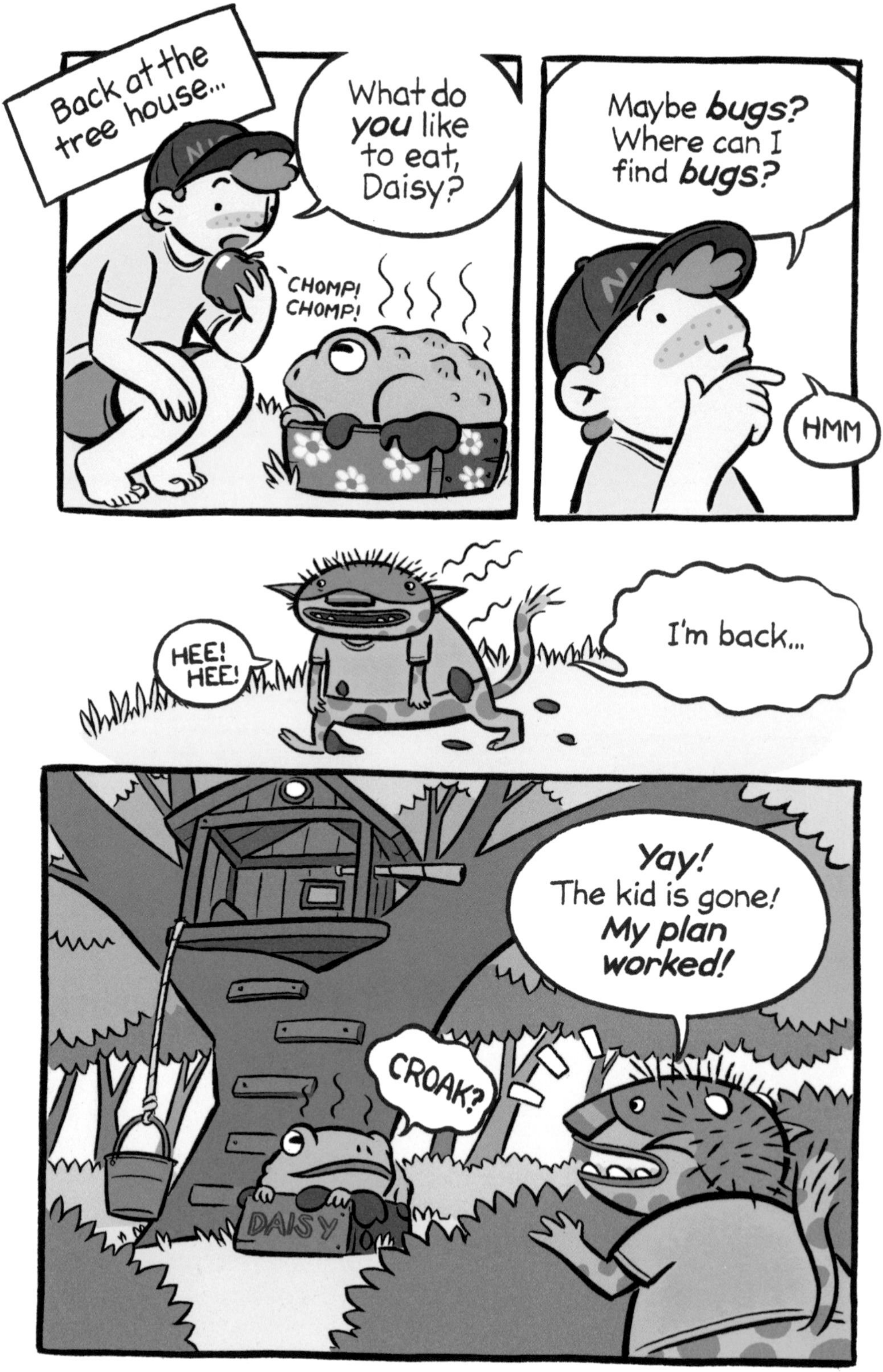

Back at the tree house...
What do you like to eat, Daisy?
CHOMP! CHOMP!
Maybe bugs? Where can I find bugs?
HMM
HEE! HEE!
I'm back...
Yay! The kid is gone! My plan worked!
CROAK?
DAISY

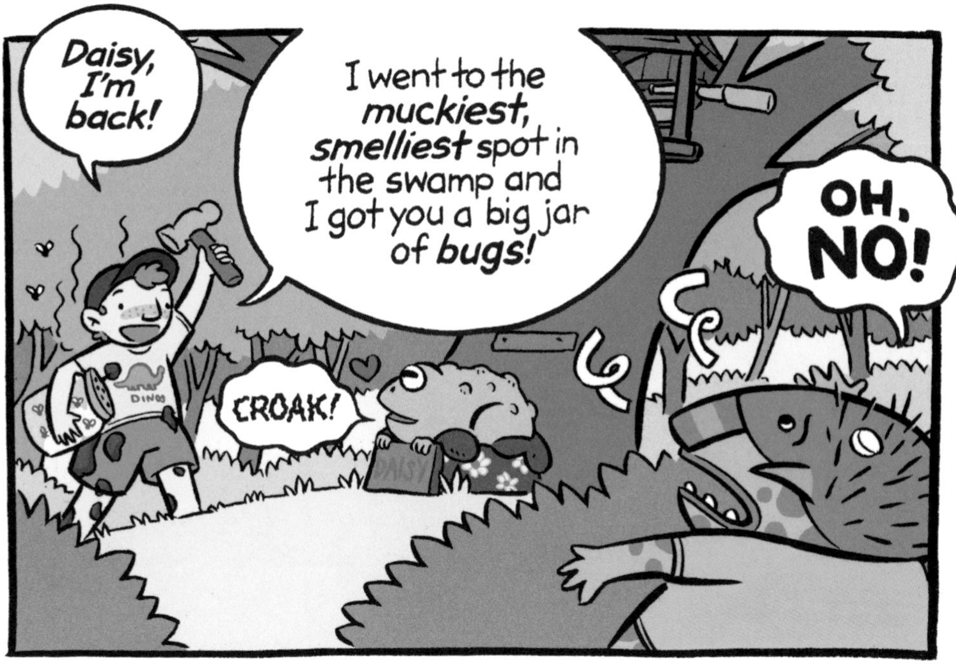

Daisy, I'm back!
I went to the muckiest, smelliest spot in the swamp and I got you a big jar of bugs!
OH, NO!
DINOS
CROAK!
DAISY

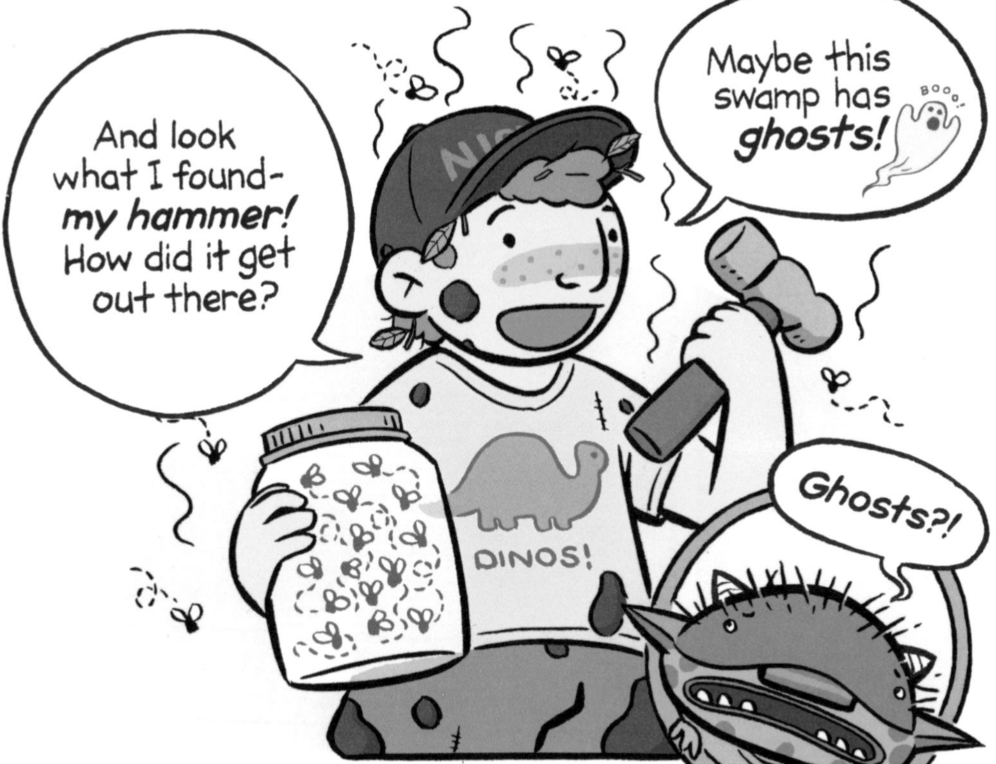

And look what I found- my hammer! How did it get out there?
Maybe this swamp has ghosts!
BOOO!
DINOS!
Ghosts?!

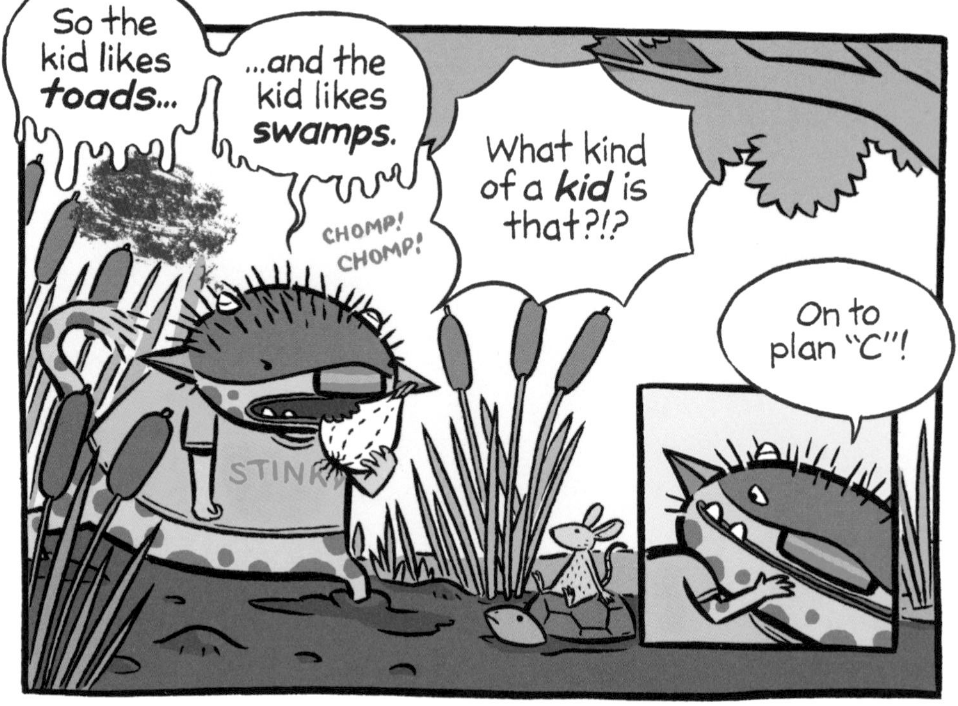

So the kid likes **toads...**
...and the kid likes **swamps.**
CHOMP! CHOMP!
STINK
What kind of a **kid** is that?!?
On to plan "C"!

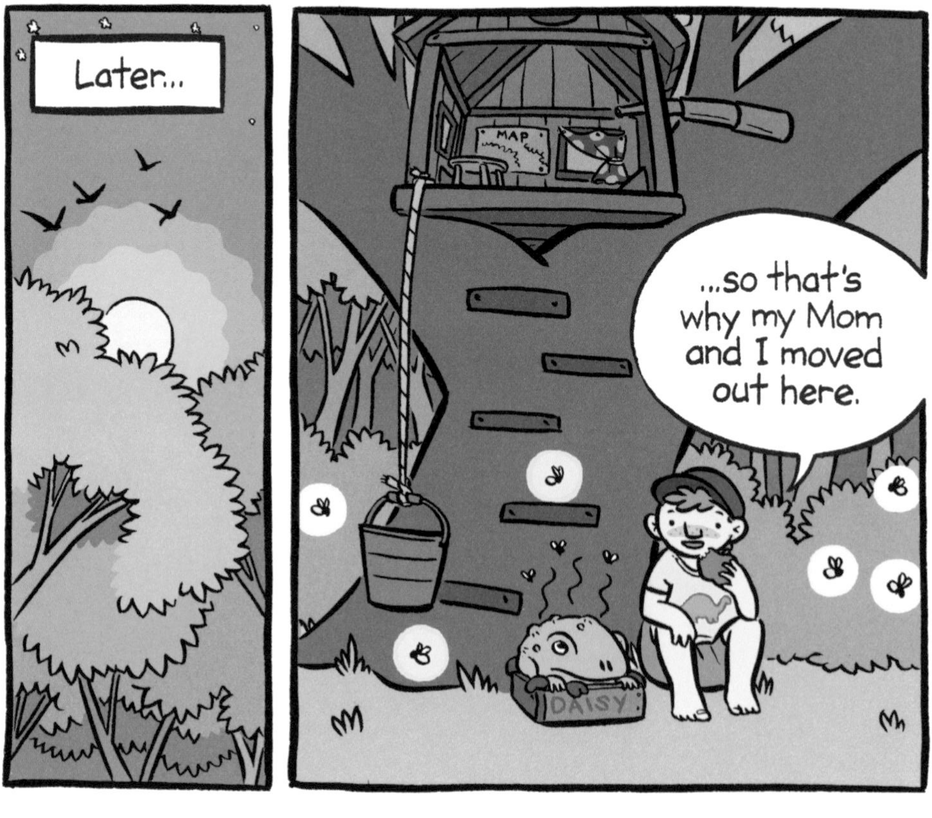

Later...
MAP
...so that's why my Mom and I moved out here.
DAISY

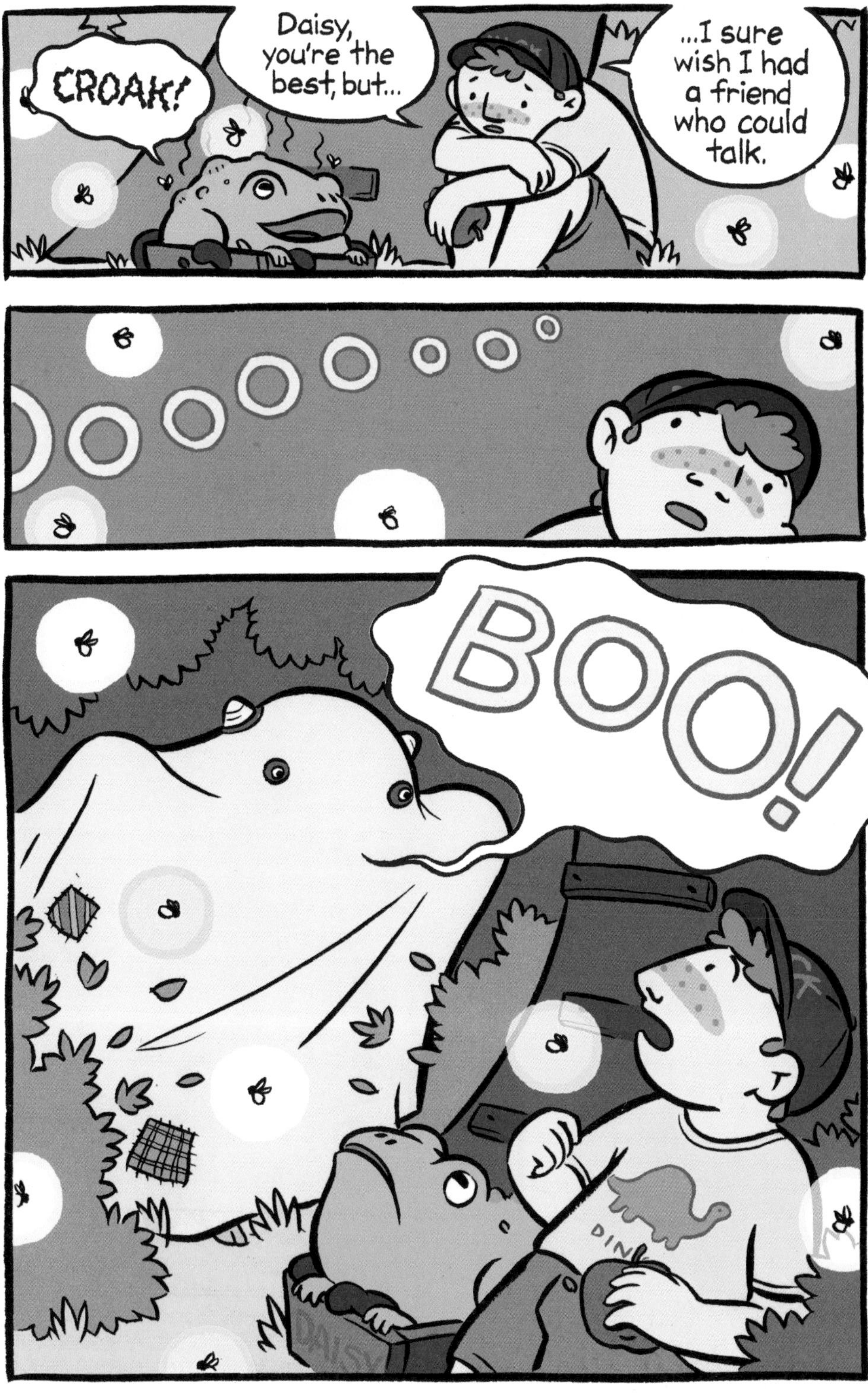
CROAK!
Daisy, you're the best, but...
...I sure wish I had a friend who could talk.
BOO!
DAISY

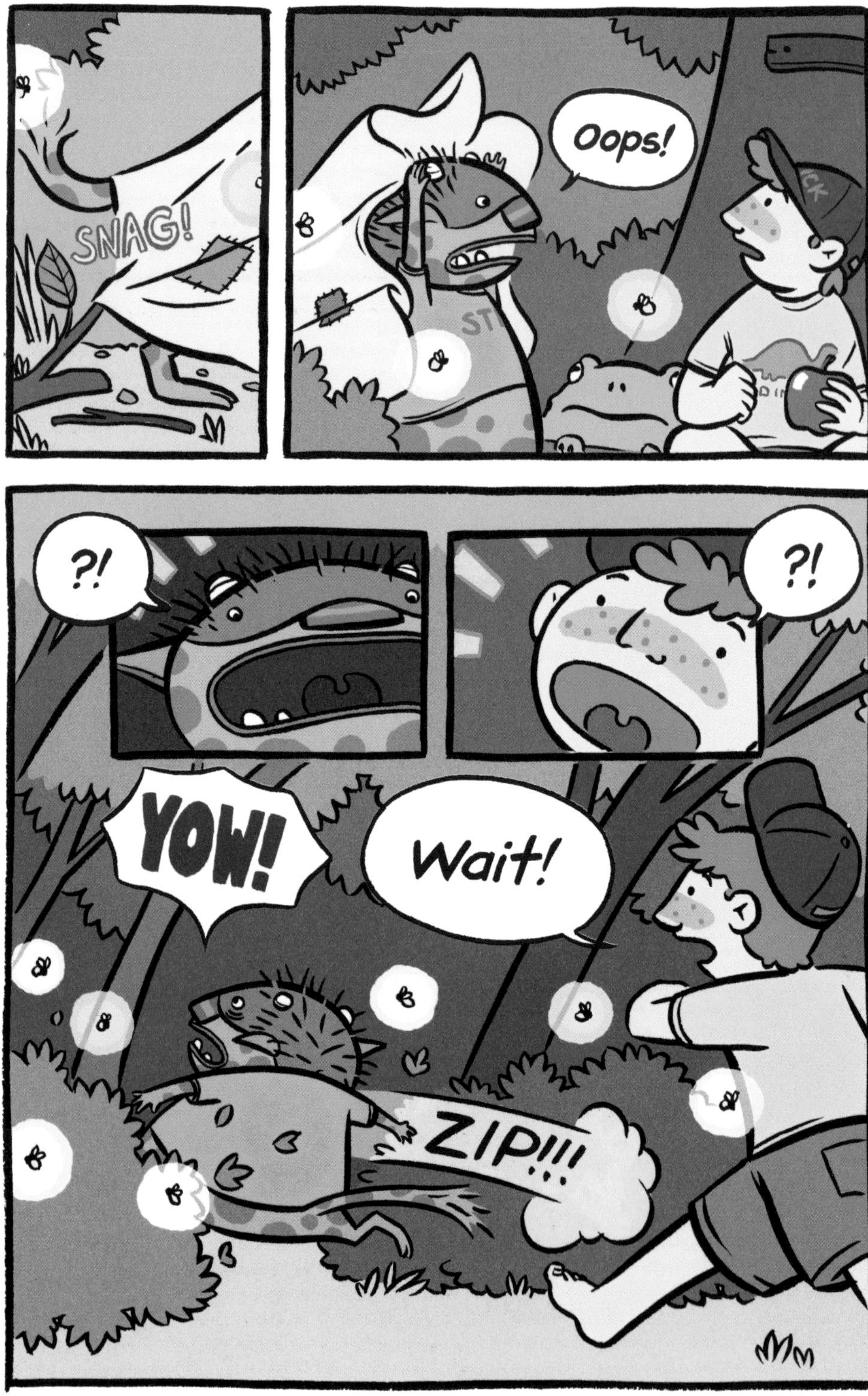
SNAG!
Oops!
?!
?!
YOW!
Wait!
ZIP!!!

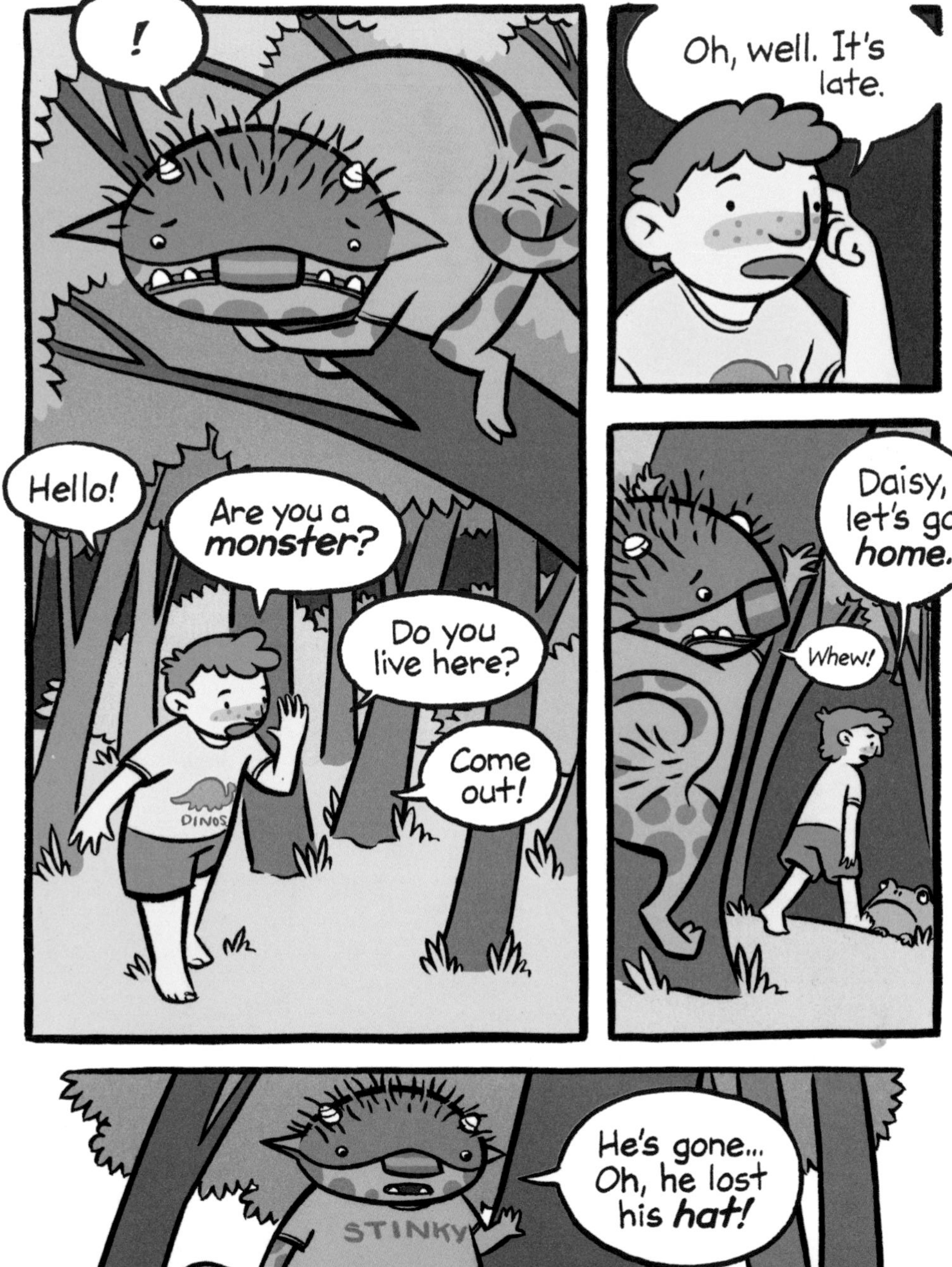

!
Hello!
Are you a **monster?**
Do you live here?
DINOS
Come out!
Oh, well. It's late.
Daisy, let's go **home.**
Whew!
STINKY
He's gone... Oh, he lost his **hat!**

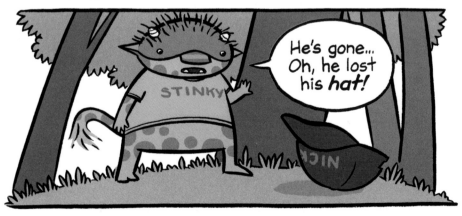

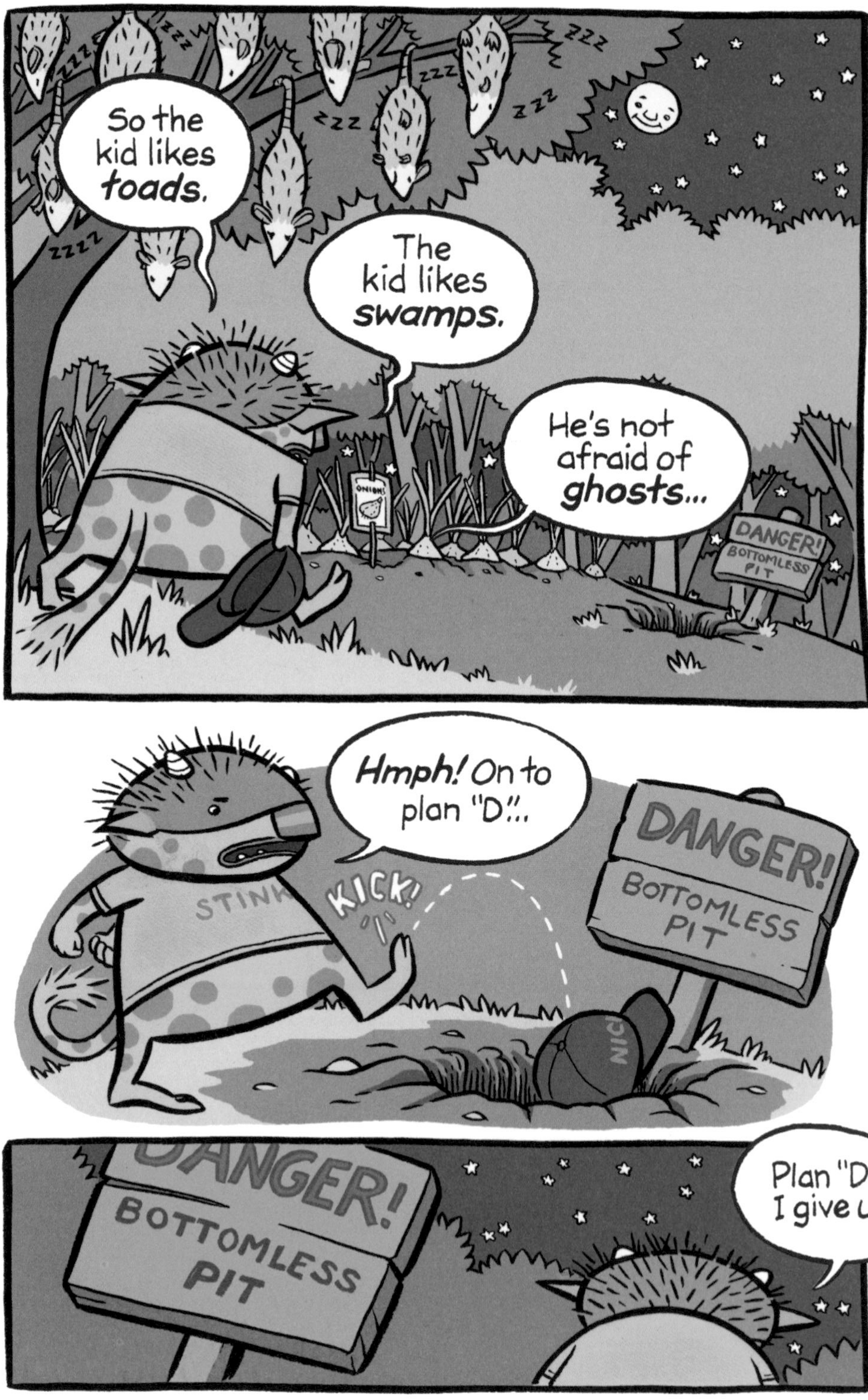
ZZZZ
ZZZ
ZZZ
ZZZ
ZZZ
ZZZ
ZZZZ
So the kid likes toads.
The kid likes swamps.
He's not afraid of ghosts...
ONIONS
DANGER! BOTTOMLESS PIT
Hmph! On to plan "D"...
STINK
KICK!
DANGER! BOTTOMLESS PIT
NIC
DANGER! BOTTOMLESS PIT
Plan "D": I give up.

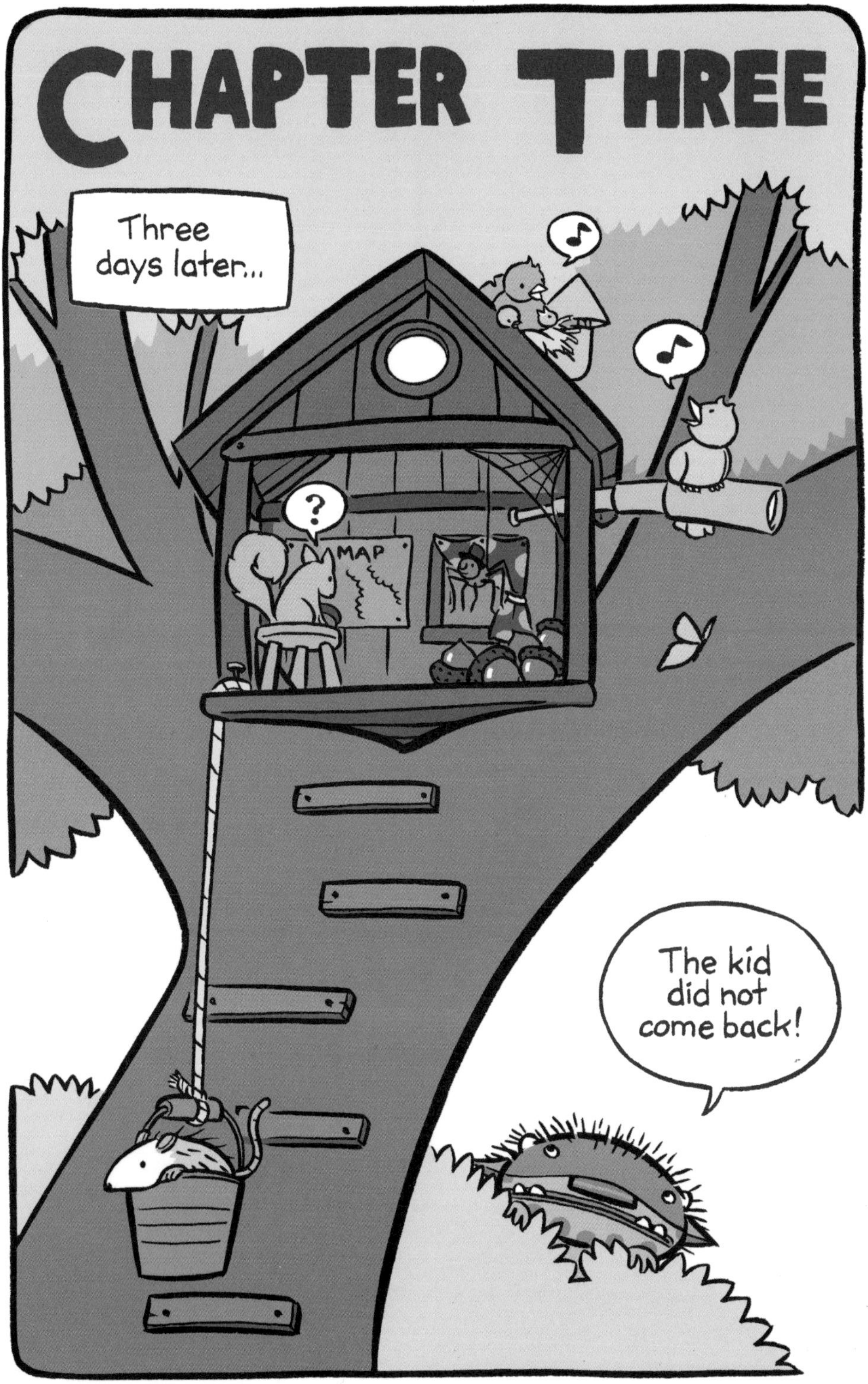
CHAPTER THREE
Three days later...
?
The kid did not come back!

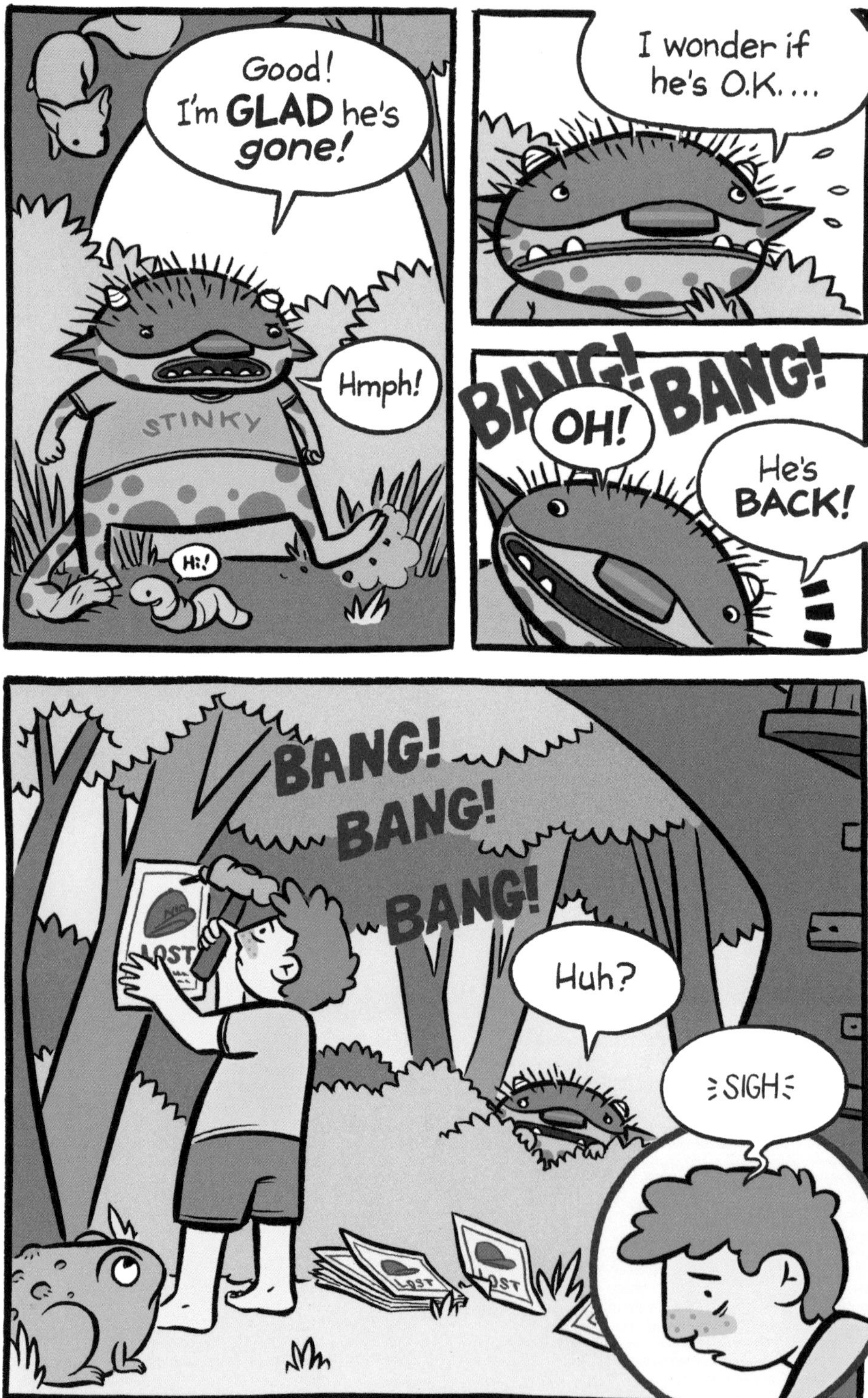
Good! I'm GLAD he's gone!
Hmph!
STINKY
Hi!
I wonder if he's O.K....
BANG! BANG!
OH!
He's BACK!
BANG! BANG! BANG!
LOST
Huh?
SIGH

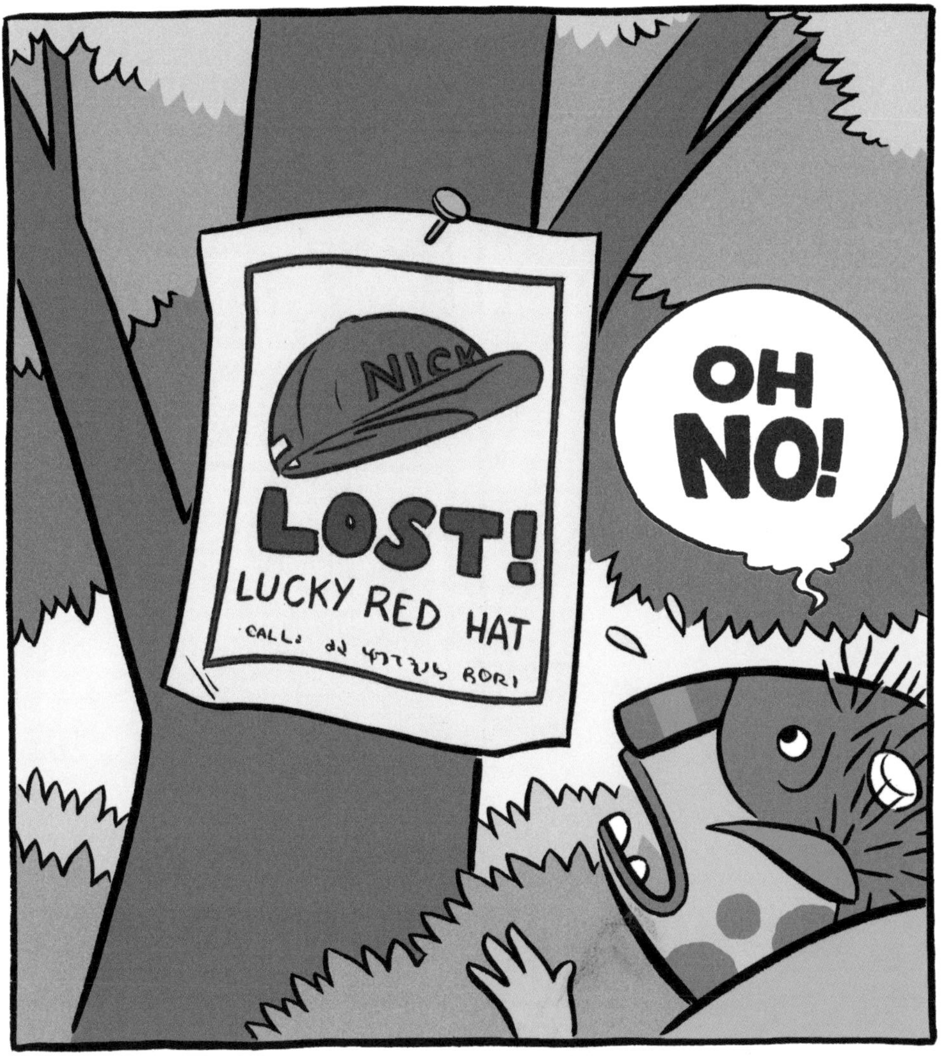
NICK
LOST!
LUCKY RED HAT
OH NO!

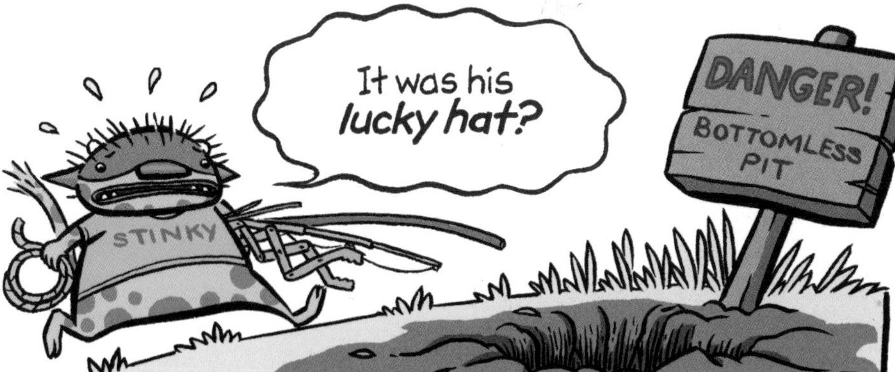
It was his *lucky hat?*
STINKY
DANGER!
BOTTOMLESS PIT

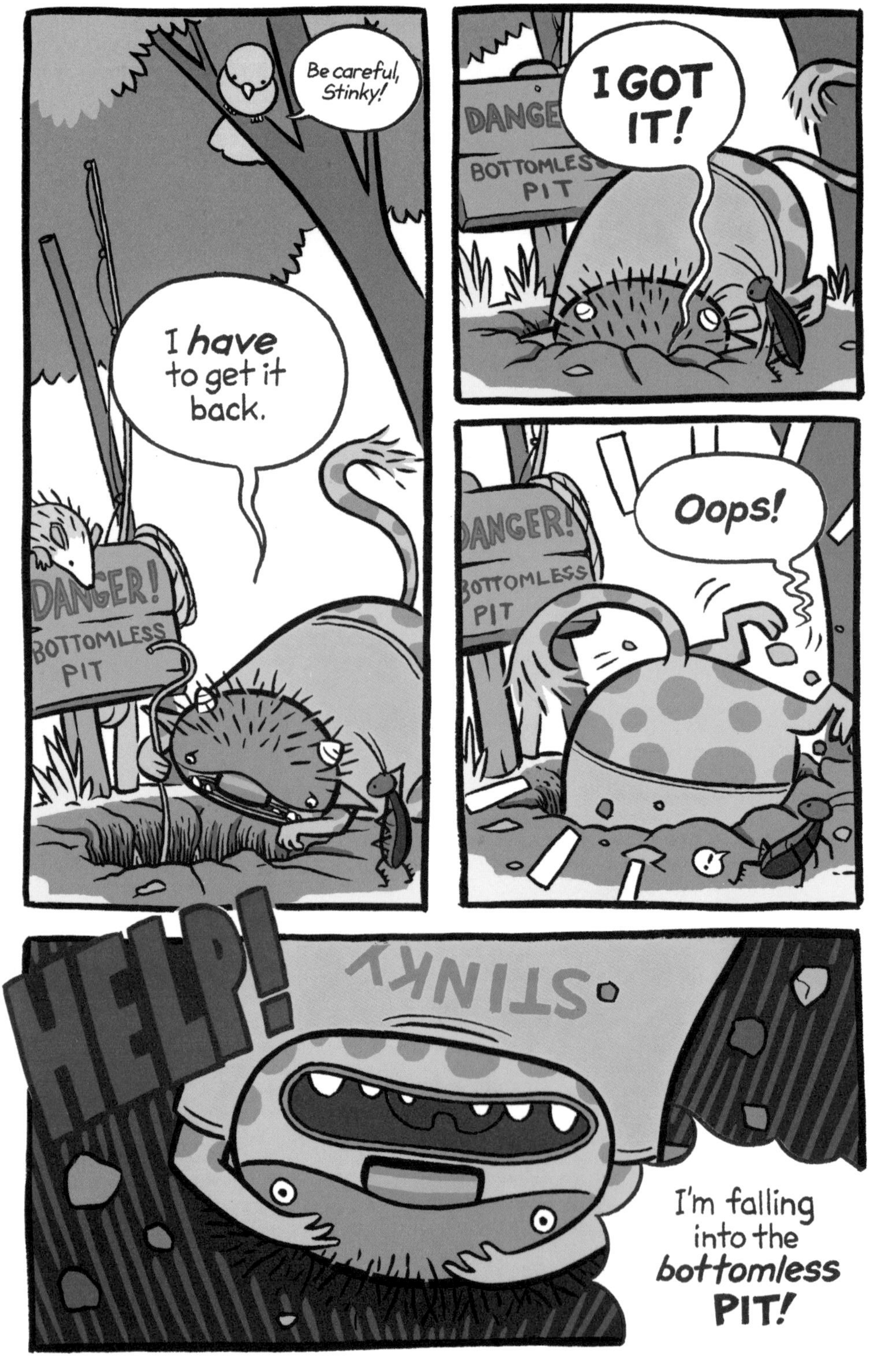
Be careful, Stinky!
I have to get it back.
DANGER! BOTTOMLESS PIT
I GOT IT!
Oops!
HELP!
STINKY
I'm falling into the bottomless PIT!

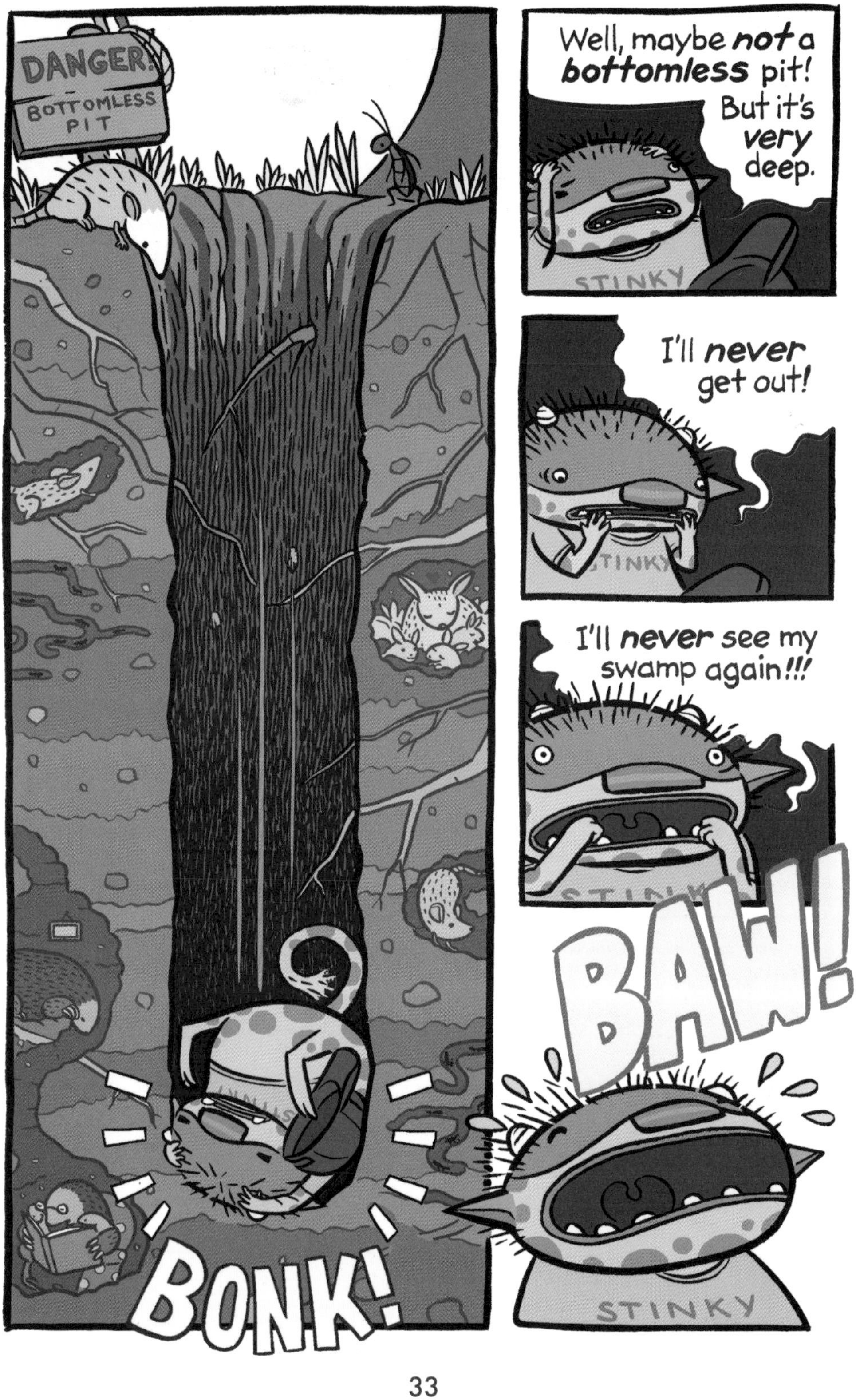
DANGER!
BOTTOMLESS PIT
STINKY
BONK!
Well, maybe not a bottomless pit! But it's very deep.
STINKY
I'll never get out!
STINKY
I'll never see my swamp again!!!
BAW!
STINKY

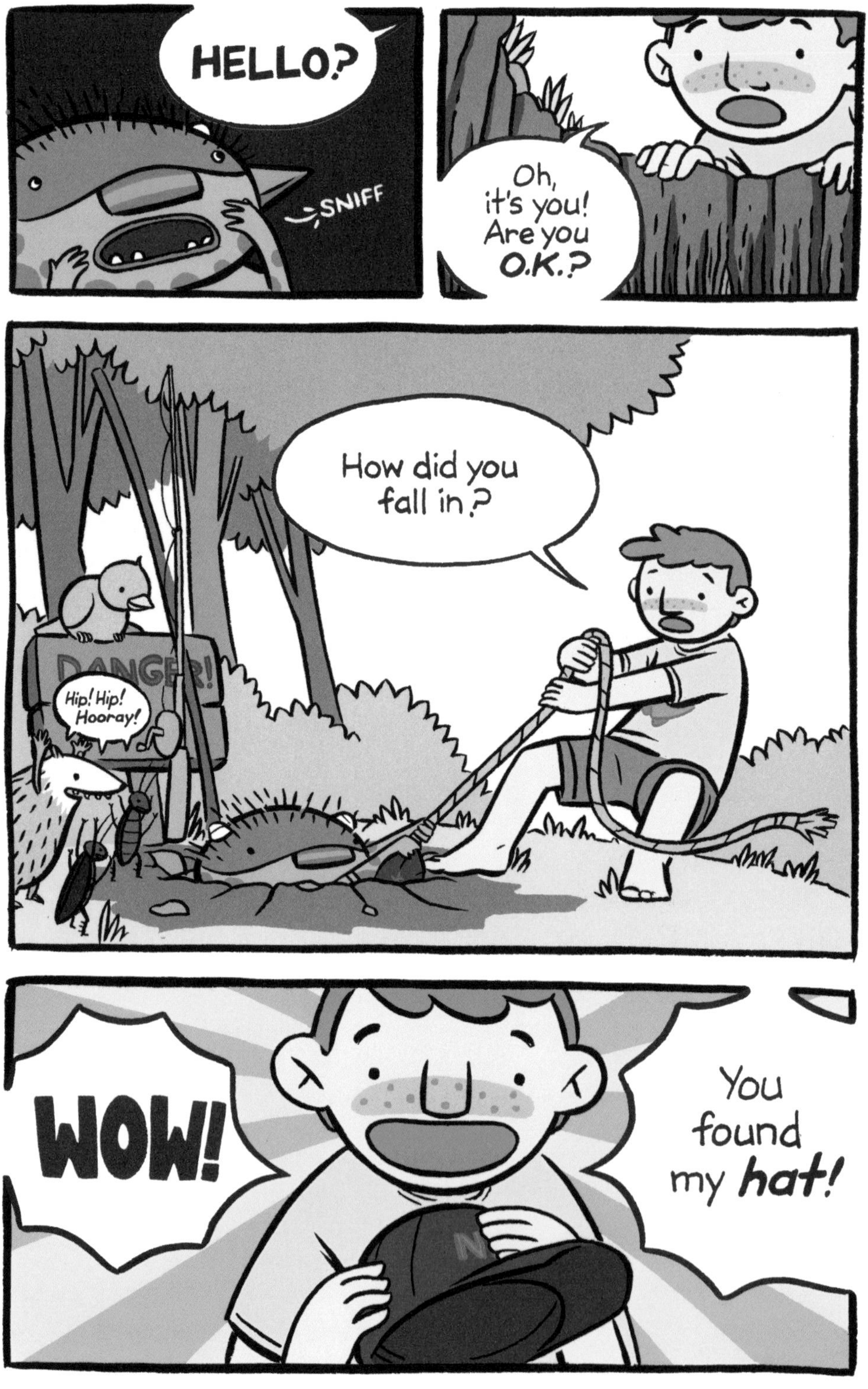
HELLO?
SNIFF
Oh, it's you! Are you O.K.?
How did you fall in?
DANGER!
Hip! Hip! Hooray!
WOW!
You found my *hat*!

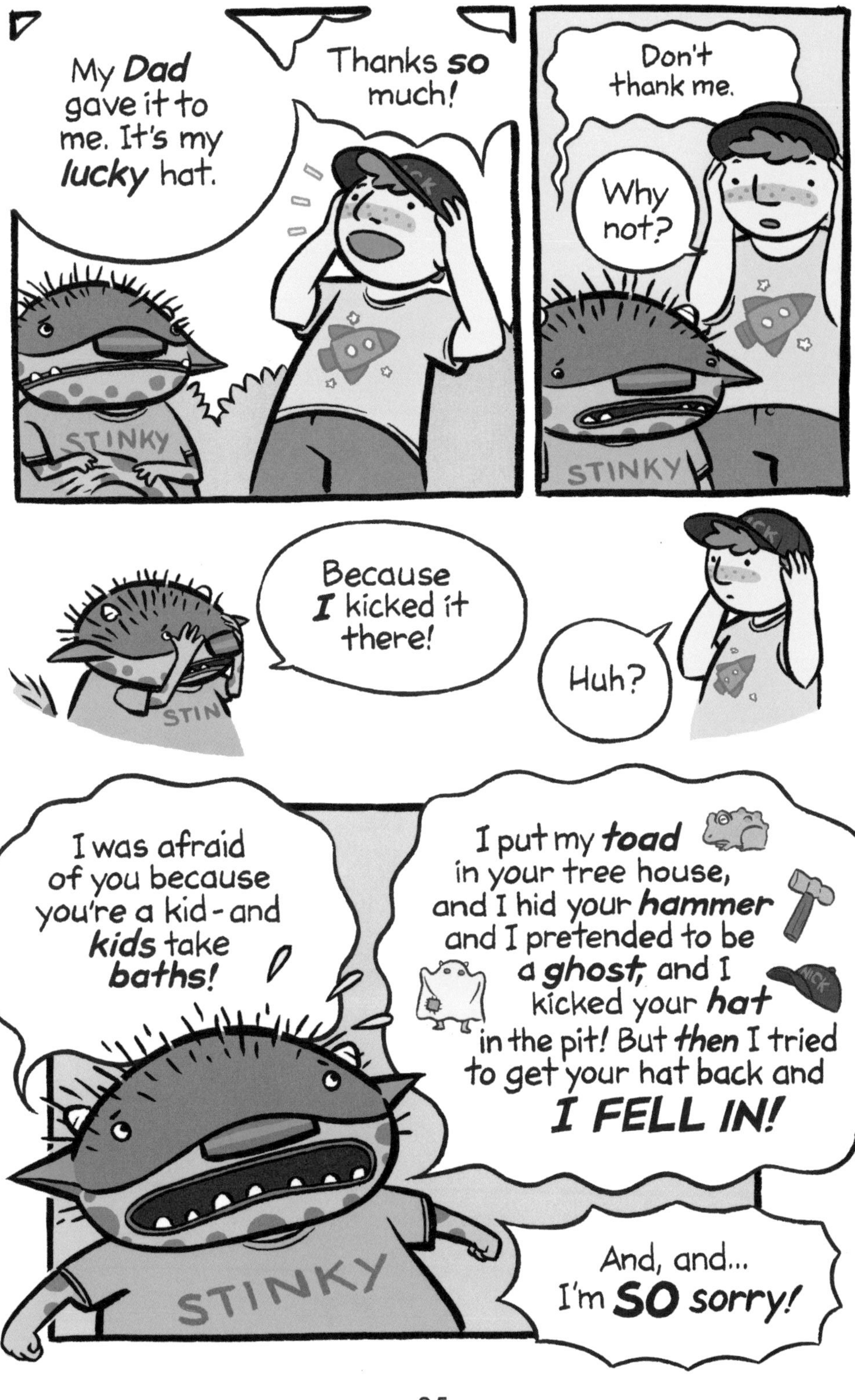
My Dad gave it to me. It's my lucky hat.
Thanks so much!
Don't thank me.
Why not?
STINKY
Because I kicked it there!
Huh?
I was afraid of you because you're a kid - and kids take baths!
I put my toad in your tree house, and I hid your hammer and I pretended to be a ghost, and I kicked your hat in the pit! But then I tried to get your hat back and I FELL IN!
And, and... I'm SO sorry!

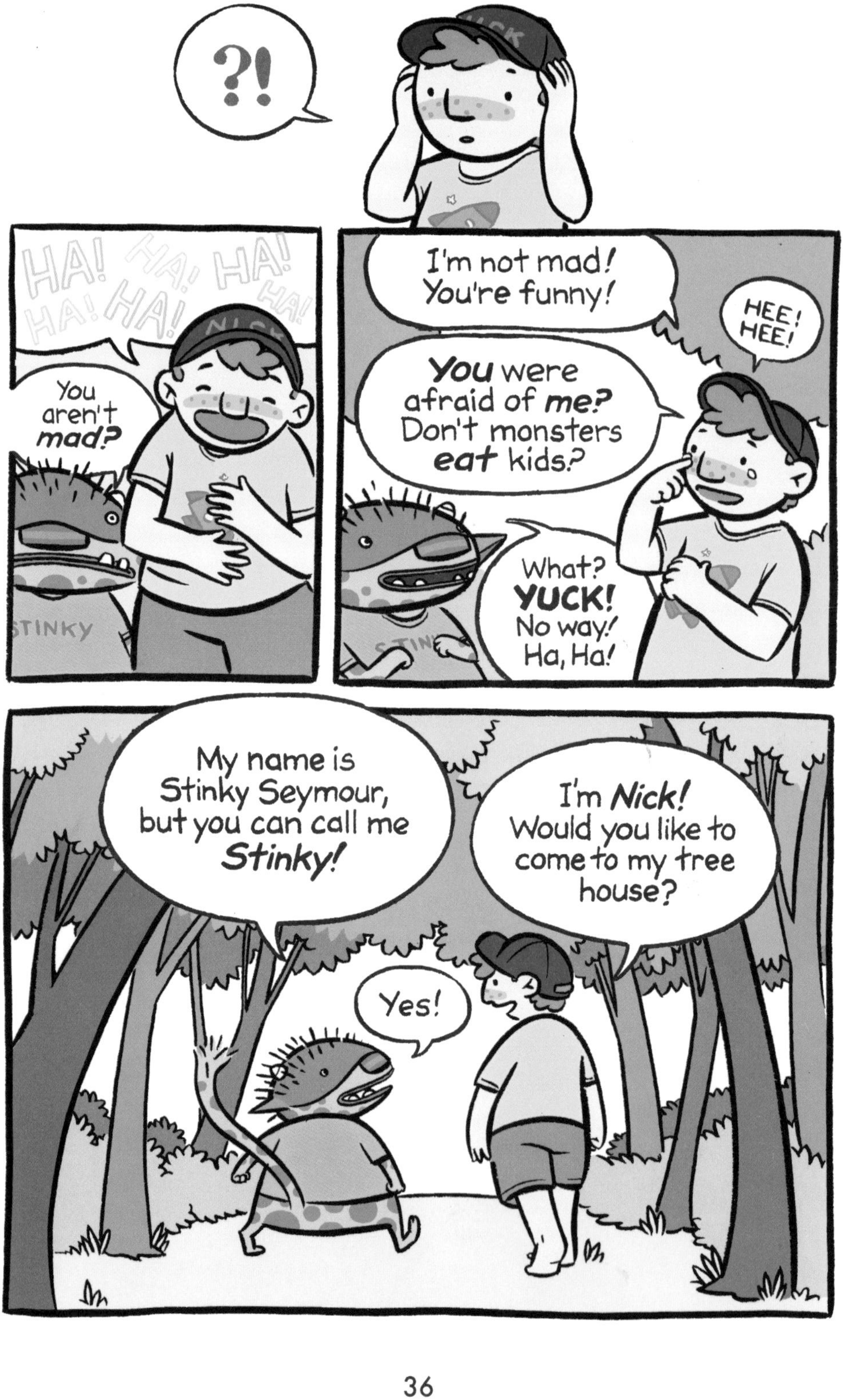
?!
HA! HA! HA! HA! HA! HA!
You aren't mad?
I'm not mad! You're funny!
HEE! HEE!
You were afraid of me? Don't monsters eat kids?
What? YUCK! No way! Ha, Ha!
My name is Stinky Seymour, but you can call me Stinky!
I'm Nick! Would you like to come to my tree house?
Yes!
NICK
STINKY

And then...

Ha! Wartbelly! I *missed* you!

CROAK!

Oh, I see! Daisy is *your* toad?

Yes! But I call her *Wartbelly.*

STIN

Let's call her **DAISY WARTBELLY!**

HA HA HA

CROAK!

Would you like an apple?

YUCK!

ER— I mean, thanks!

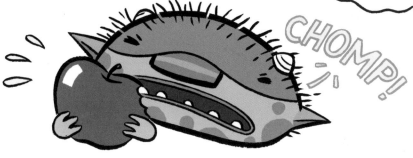

CHOMP!

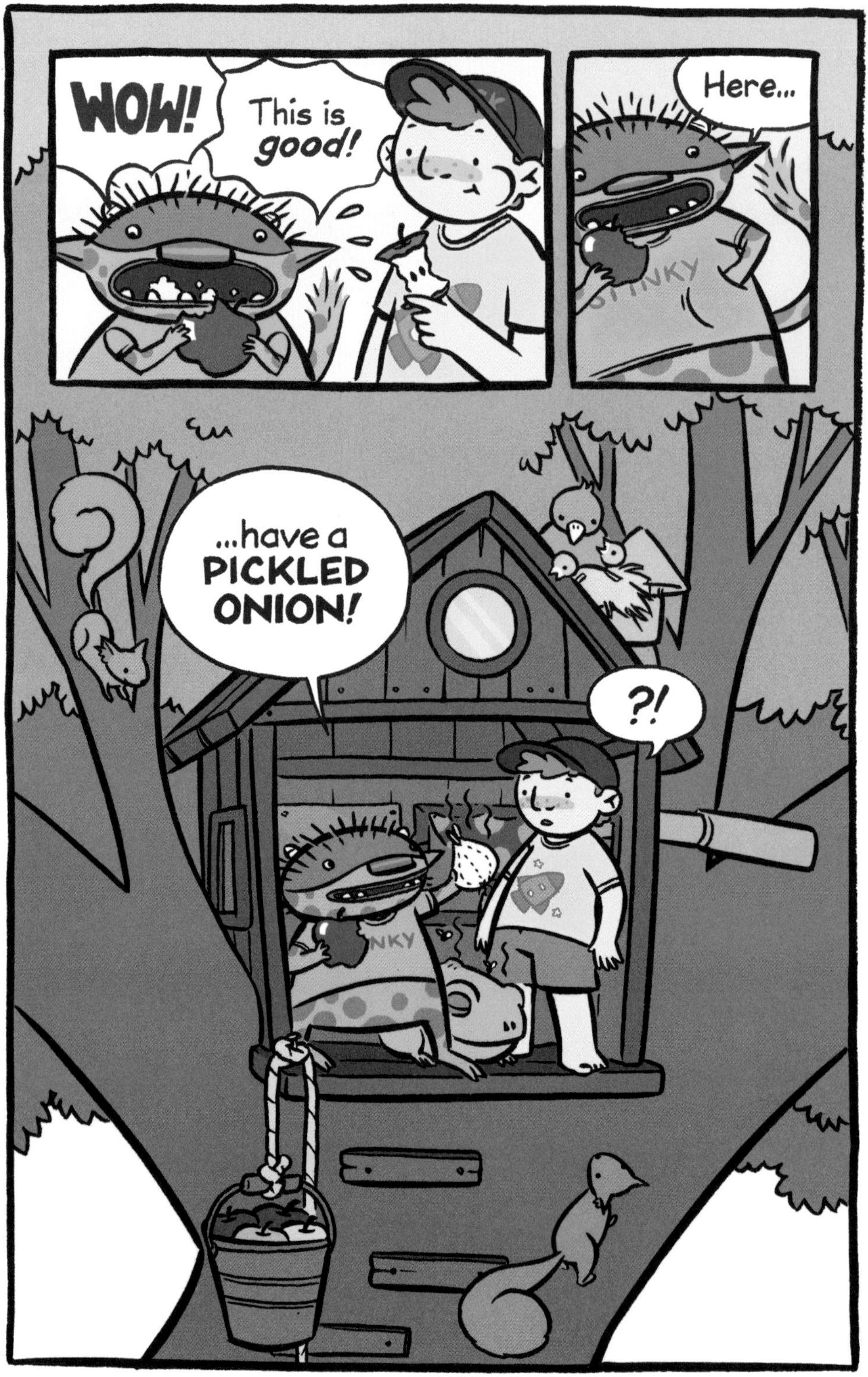
WOW!
This is *good!*
Here...
STINKY
...have a PICKLED ONION!
?!

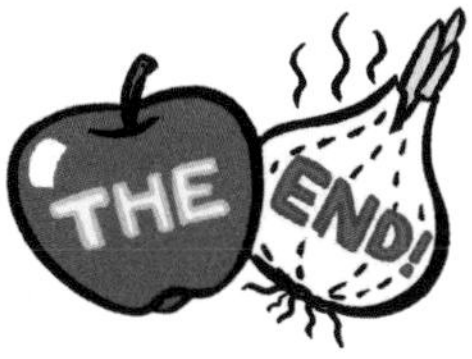
THE
END!

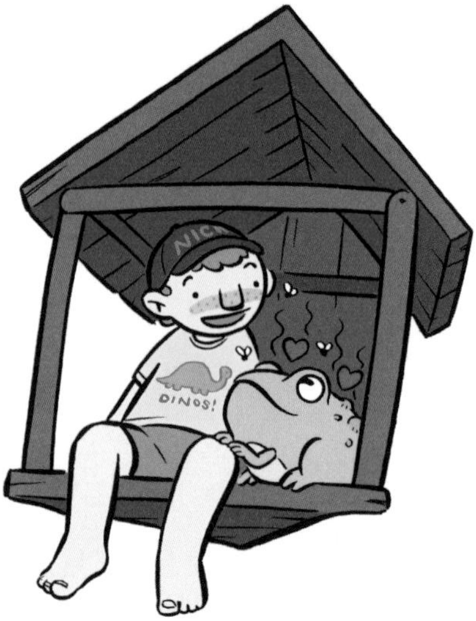
DINOS!

ABOUT THE AUTHOR

ELEANOR DAVIS grew up in Tucson, Arizona. Instead of going out in the hot sun to play and make friends, she stayed alone in her room, drawing. She started working on *Stinky*, her first published children's book, while still a student at the Savannah College of Art and Design. Now, only 25 years old, she's widely praised as one of the coolest artists on the new comics scene.

She lives in Athens, Georgia, with her boyfriend (who is also a cartoonist) and three cats (who are not).

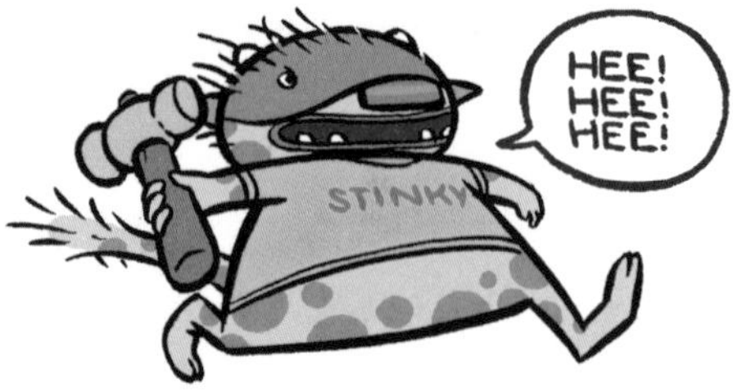
STINKY
HEE! HEE! HEE!

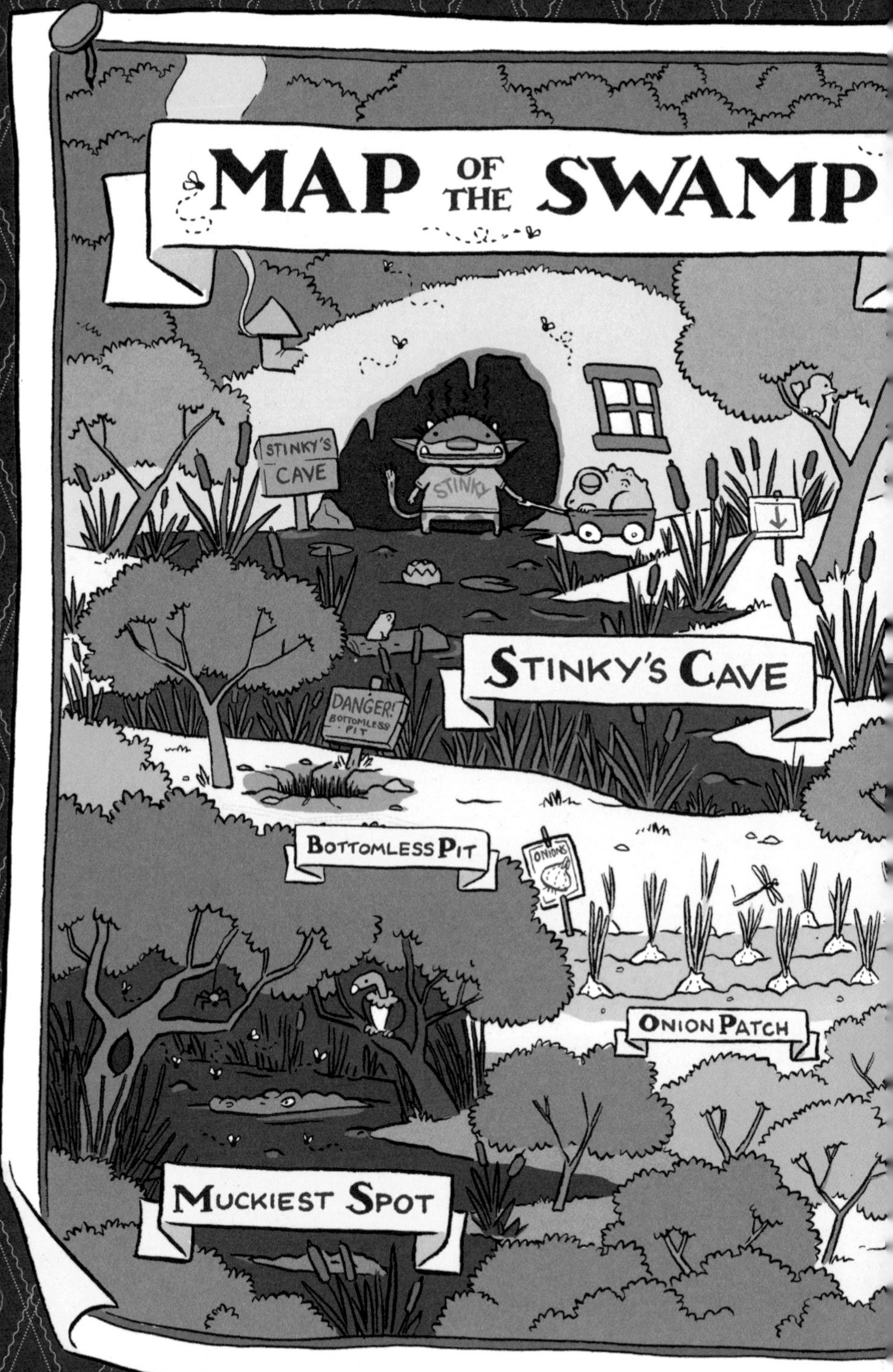
MAP OF THE SWAMP
STINKY'S CAVE
STINKY
STINKY'S CAVE
DANGER! BOTTOMLESS PIT
BOTTOMLESS PIT
ONIONS
ONION PATCH
MUCKIEST SPOT